To Tom

...e
...s!
x

...a, Mark, Jamie,
Luke + Pollyanna
x

ELATED BY DETAILS

Award-winning Short Stories

Adam Freedman

ELATED BY DETAILS

Award-winning Short Stories

Adam Freedman

Mayhaven Publishing

Mayhaven Publishing
PO Box 557
Mahomet, IL 61853

All rights reserved
This is a work of fiction

First Edition-First Printing
Copyright © 2003 Adam Freedman

Cover Art - *Sightlines* © Alexi Worth
Courtesy of the artist and Bill Maynes Gallery, New York
LOC: # 2003112296
ISBN: 1-878044-99-0
Printed in Canada

For My Parents

Acknowledgments

Many thanks to my agent, Geri Thoma, and to Doris Wenzel of Mayhaven Publishing, for their professional guidance and support. I am also grateful for the encouragement of my family, co-workers at Schulte Roth & Zabel, and friends, especially Bart Aronson, Erika Belsey, Eric Berg, Sheri Berman, Ian Jacobs, Rob Long, Tim Naftali, Gideon Rose, Dan Staley, Anne and Erik Tozzi, Alexi Worth, Andrea Yao-Berg, and Paula and Fareed Zakaria, to name a few. Eternal gratitude to my fiancé, Kathleen Walsh, for her enthusiasm—and patience.

Contents

BROKER 9
ELATED BY DETAILS 16
ABROAD AT CHRISTMAS 38
THE SMELL OF SUCCESS 57
THE SECRET PASSION OF AN ARTIST 93
A REGULAR DON JUAN 98
PLODGETT REVISITED 120
THE BED 138
THE MAGIC KINGDOM 147
JUSTICE AFTER A FASHION 160
THE EDUCATION OF ANDREW PEARLSTEIN 165
FOLLOW THE BURSTING BUBBLE 188

BROKER

Having treated me to a sound drubbing in the stock market, bond market, and futures market, my broker tried to get me into the one market left—the marriage market.

"The marriage market," said my broker, Bubbles Pilferheimer, "is a very smart play at the moment." She was trying to fix me up with another of her luckless clients.

"I can't afford marriage," I said.

"You're looking at this the wrong way, Sidney," she said. "In a downturn, you can't afford not to be married. This is a time for pooling resources, family values, nesting, and all that crap. Wait 'till you meet this woman I have in mind!"

"I appreciate the thought, Bubbles," I said, "but isn't this a little beyond the call of duty for a broker?"

"Brokers live by word-of-mouth, Sidney. I want you to say nice things about me."

"I do say nice things. For example: you've never caused me any tax trouble."

"You know what, Sidney? I think you'd like yourself better if you had a good woman at your side. I'm telling you, this woman is blue chip."

To get Bubbles off my back, I took the woman—Oprah was her name—out on a date. She was a high-strung blond who told me about a recurring dream she was having. The dream involved scuba diving and coral reefs and may or may not have been a coded message. In any event, we didn't "click," as they say, and I failed to call her again.

"I'm sorry to hear that," said Bubbles the following week. "But to be totally frank, Sidney, I don't think the two of you were right for each other. That's why this is such a fantastic opportunity for you. I have this client—"

Unfortunately, things did not go any better with Sally; or with Jesse, the next two women with whom Bubbles fixed me up. It was not a problem of physical attraction. Sally was a voluptuous Italian-American; Jesse, a long-legged wannabe model. Even Oprah had had a certain nervy appeal.

No, my objection to Oprah, Sally, and Jesse lay elsewhere. You see, I am a man with very particular tastes. In happier times, when Bubbles was steering me into hot biotech start-ups and surging dot-coms, I spent months preparing myself for the harvest of cash I would soon be

Elated By Details

reaping. With diligent research, I learned the best vintages for Chateau Petrus, the name of the concierge at the Paris Ritz, and the strengths and weaknesses of Savile Row tailors.

When I was ready to start spending my fortune, I asked Bubbles: "Shouldn't I sell and take some profits?"

"What's the rush?" Bubbles had said. "The market's got 'uge upside potential. And I mean 'uge with a capital U."

"Bubbles," I pleaded, "I want to buy things! I want to start living life!"

"Nobody's stopping you, Sidney. If you see something you like—buy it! Just use credit! You can't lose in this market."

Bubbles, of course, had been mistaken. I was not bitter, however, even though I ended up losing my life savings in the crash that followed. I'm an optimist by nature, and I still dreamed of a life filled with the finer things. But that life was not to be had with Oprah, Sally, or Jesse. They were all in the same boat as me — poor clients of Bubbles.

I found myself in Bubbles' office one day. I had to get her signature on various papers relating to my personal bankruptcy. She was a robust woman with wavy brown hair. She favored navy business suits and colorful silk scarves. Her face, in rare moments of repose, was rather pretty. At other times, it seemed to consist entirely of teeth.

At the news of my bankruptcy, Bubbles shook her head sadly. "You know what's funny? It's not even that I mind losing the commissions. I just wish things would have worked out for you, romance-wise."

"Times are tough, Bubbles."

She looked through her Rolodex. "It's no use," she said. "I only know one other single woman — myself." She laughed with a nasal hee-haw. "But hey, why not go a little crazy? It's almost quitting time around her, and I could use a drink. Are you free?"

"Practically."

And so began my whirlwind courtship of Bubbles Pilferheimer. It was an odd courtship, since she paid for everything — but I soon got over that. We sat in high-end bars, perusing *Cosmopolitan* over a couple of Rusty Nails, and we sat in low-end bars perusing a couple of rusty nails over Cosmopolitans. It was nuts, but we didn't care what other people thought: romance was in the air. Bubbles took me to lavish dinners, and suggested we have each other for dessert. But I guarded my virtue, tightening my chastity belt even as I loosened my real belt.

One night, Bubbles took me to a party given by some of her friends from Wall Street. We stood arm-in-arm, talking to a similarly besotted couple, the male half of which said: "*We* met each other through mutual friends. What about you guys?"

"We met through mutual funds," I said.

I felt distinctly out of my league in this world of brokers and investment bankers. Later, at the same party, a couple of tough-talking men in bright ties struck up a conversation, introducing themselves as "I-bankers." I did not volunteer my own profession. How could I admit that I was nothing

Elated By Details

but a lowly clerk in the Manhattan Organ Bank? But the question inevitably came up: "So, what do you do, Sidney?"

"I'm an eye-banker," I said sadly.

"Way to go!" they both exclaimed, offering me the "high five."

Still, I felt the evening had been a failure. As Bubbles walked me to my door, she picked up on my air of melancholy with her customary tact. "Why are you being such a picklepuss?" she said, pushing me over the threshold of my apartment.

"I don't know where I fit in your world," I said. She had followed me inside and shut the door behind us. "When it comes to finance, all I've ever done is lose my shirt."

She grabbed me by the chastity belt. "I think it's time to lose the pants, too."

We were married in a civil ceremony. Bubbles had been married before. Well married, too, for she had ended up with substantial assets from the first husband, including a baronial estate located atop the highest hill in Scarsdale. I moved to Scarsdale, and spent some of the happiest months of my life in that house.

In those heady days, I was overwhelmed by Bubbles' generosity. "Darling," I said to her, as we sat up one night making another round of revisions to her will, "shouldn't you leave something for your parents? Or your poor siblings?"

I tried, I really did, but she wouldn't have it. "I want you to have everything," she said, redolent with emotion.

She would have signed that version of the will, too, had she been able to keep the pen steady as she wept. I, too, became emotional when it came to matters of estate planning. I told Bubbles I didn't know how I would carry on if she were to leave this world. I suppose that's why she took out such a generous life insurance policy, naming me as the sole beneficiary.

Silly Bubbles! She would never have time for the breakfast I would cook her, but would instead bid me farewell with a peck on the cheek as she rushed out to the car. I would stay and potter around the house — well, there was no point staying on at Organ Bank, was there? It got lonely when Bubbles went away to visit clients on the West Coast, as she often did. That's why I renewed my acquaintance with Oprah, Sally and Jesse, who would visit me when Bubbles was away. Sometimes one of them would even stay the night. Very occasionally, two of them would stay the night. It was a great comfort to me.

You can't really appreciate the loneliness of that house unless you consider how *big* it was! It was the kind of house that cried out for heavy Jacobean furnishings, hand-loomed Persian rugs, and Old Master canvases. Instead, Bubbles, who was getting a bit bossy in her control over the purse strings, insisted on filling the place up with day-glow modern art, "vintage" jukeboxes, and suchlike bric-a-brac. We argued for some time over my plan to convert the basement into a wine cellar, but in the end Bubbles had to have her way, didn't she? It remained a "rec" room.

Elated By Details

But looking back, I would have all those arguments again, a thousand times over, if I could just have my Bubbles back. I don't know how many times I told her to get those brakes fixed! When I heard the car squeal uncontrollably down our hill it was as though my own life was passing before my eyes. I suppose I should take some comfort in the fact that Bubbles, unbeknownst to me, had something of a death wish. The coroner tells me there were small traces of arsenic in her blood, as though she were slowly poisoning herself. Maybe that's why she never got those brakes fixed.

Me? I'm going to be fine. During the past few days of sitting shiva, Oprah, Sally and Jesse have been at my side, day and night. With their kind help, I have started to put the pieces of my life back together.

And that, officer, is all I have to say about my wife's death.

ELATED BY DETAILS

I would never have met Professor Clapham had it not been for my high school's policy of allowing seniors to cut class — provided they were going to a college recruiting presentation.

My debate partner, Les Calley, and I spent our senior year racking up recruiting pitches the way James Bond accumulated sexual conquests. We would meet in the morning at the Guidance Office to check out the day's schedule; calculating which of the presentations coincided with our most hated classes. Because our little corner of North Shore Chicago had reasonably good schools, there was a lavish array of colleges vying for our parents' money.

By October, Les and I were hitting our stride. On the day of our AP History quiz, we discovered an insatiable

Elated By Details

desire to learn more about the four-year colleges of Wisconsin, several of which were putting on presentations in the school auditorium. "Go ahead," our history teacher, Mr. Button, said as he signed the hall passes. "But I'm giving you a take-home exam to make up for this. Forty minutes, closed book. You're on the honor system, understand?"

"Yes," we said in unison, thinking: why not just give us an "A" and have done with it? We bounded off to the auditorium light hearted with the knowledge that these presentations would take up most of the afternoon.

The recruiting director from the University of Western Wisconsin — decked out in a rectangular knit tie, topsiders, and tweed jacket — was making the most of slender material. "The UWW," he declared, "has the leading paper-mill engineering department in the country!"

I whispered in Les' ear and he, being bolder than I, raised his hand. "What's so complicated about pepper mills? I mean, don't you just put the peppercorns in the top and—"

"It's not pepper, it's—"

I tried to suppress a giggle, which only succeeded in egging Les on, for this sort of thing was our stock-in-trade. "And what about salt shaker engineering?" he continued. "Do you have to go to a different school for that?"

"It's *paper* mill," said the recruiting director, who was to be commended for not killing the both of us.

"Geez, why didn't you say so?" said Les. At this, my

suppressed laughter turned into a full-fledged guffaw. This inability to control my own giggles had always kept me from becoming a leading class clown. I was, however, valued as a source of "material" in the way of puns and other word plays that Les put to good use. Our favorite was the palindrome, which we had learned in English class the previous year. But new palindromes were difficult to compose, and the established ones — "A man, a plan, a canal, Panama" — ceased to be amusing after a few go-rounds. So, Les and I developed our own unique specialty: the faux palindrome; that is, a phrase that sounds as though it might be a palindrome, but in fact is not — "Lulu ruined our luau".

"If I may continue," the recruiting director said wearily, "in addition to its *paper mill* engineering department, the UWW also offers undergraduates a full program of liberal arts. I take it," he said with a ghost of a sneer, "that you scholars are interested in the liberal arts?"

"Liberal arts startle librarians," I said, to Les' appreciative snort.

Despite these occasional flights of Noel Cowardice, we sat through most of the recruiting pitches in a glassy silence. Still, the presentations served their main purpose, which was to bring us that much closer to three o'clock. I would fall into the same mindset years later when, working at a law firm, I found myself secretly cheering for any of the "boring" civic duties — voting, blood drives, fire drills — that would allow me to skip out of the office with impunity for a precious hour or two.

Elated By Details

Attending the recruiting pitches also gave me ammunition to counter my father's regular injunctions to do something about my future; his constant nagging insistence that I continue to get good grades, that I figure out my future career path, that I deduce the best college major to pursue that career, and that I apply to the best college to pursue that major. Or at least, that was the upshot of it all. What my father actually said, through a haze of pipe smoke, was "have you sorted out college yet?" The rest was sort of implied.

Before I could answer my father, he would usually turn his attention back to whatever medical journal he was reading. Occasionally, he would listen long enough for me to tell him about some college I was considering.

"Do they offer pre-med courses?" was his only follow-up question.

"I guess," I would say. *Go ahead; tell me you want me to become a doctor. Just tell me.*

"Oh well, I'm sure you'll sort something out. Just use your best judgment."

The last presentation of the afternoon was St. Oscar's, a small college near Green Bay, and it was something of a sensation. Rather than send a recruiting officer, St. Oscar's sent a real live professor to give a 'guest lecture.'

"I'm going to talk about the Renaissance today," Professor Clapham announced. He was tall and broad shouldered, with a grizzled beard that gave him an impish quality, despite his height. "Can anyone tell me when the

Renaissance began?"

"Umm, it was, like, after the Middle Ages, right?" said one of the pre-college puddings.

"Very good," said Professor Clapham, "except that answer doesn't tell me anything. What did it mean for the Middle Ages to end? What did it mean for the Renaissance to begin?"

"The Middle Ages made sages dim," I said to Les.

"Yes?" said the professor, fixing on me. "You are Mister—?"

"Blankenship. Josh Blankenship."

"Splendid. Mr. Blankensop has an observation?"

"Blankensop!" cried the football and hockey players. Professor Clapham quieted them down, which gave me just enough time to pull a rabbit out of my hat.

"Isn't this all just semantics?" I said. "Whether we call it 'Middle Ages' or 'Renaissance' won't change what happened, it just makes people see it a certain way. It's like calling the Civil War the 'War for Southern Independence.'"

"Interesting point," the professor conceded. "But since we cannot avoid using words, we cannot avoid making those kinds of choices. We cannot say when something 'begins' until we have defined what that 'something' is. A lot of people say that life begins at forty. Does that mean I could kill any of you, since you aren't technically alive yet?"

The auditorium buzzed with suddenly stimulated minds. Hands were raised and the rest of the hour passed in a pleasant series of exchanges, to which Les and I made several

Elated By Details

non-ironic contributions. After the lecture, Les and I drifted to the front of the class where the professor was entertaining questions about St. Oscar's. I had no interest in spending four years in rural Wisconsin; my sights were already set on an imaginary New England campus, where I would wear tweed jackets and smoke a pipe through a permanent autumn. Still, I felt I had earned the right to hobnob with Clapham, having survived the thrust and parry of his real-life college lecture.

"Well, Mr. Blankenship," the professor said, pulling his blazer off of the back of a chair, "you appear to be educable."

I did not disagree. We had a little chat, during which it transpired that Clapham was staying in Chicago, where he was taking a group of St. Oscar's students around to the Newberry Library, Art Institute, Lyric Opera, and such cultural sites that were old hat to North Shore boys like myself.

"I'm preparing young men and women to make charming cocktail conversation," Professor Clapham said. I laughed knowingly, as one who shared the professor's disdain for such superficialities. Clapham invited Les and me to come downtown and eat pizza with the St. Oscar's crowd on Friday.

I asked if St. Oscar's wasn't, like, a religious school?

"You shouldn't use the word 'like' as a conversational crutch," he said, stroking his beard. "You're too smart for that. In any event, it is true that St. O's was founded as a Catholic college, but now it is officially secular — open to all. However," he added vaguely, "we do try to maintain some traditional values. Why not meet some students? Come for the intellectual refreshment."

"Stay for the pizza!" said Les.

"Sure," I said.

"Sure," said Les.

"I think you both mean, 'yes, thank you,' don't you?"

"Oh yeah," we said, feeling uncharacteristically humble.

* * *

That Friday, I asked for the car keys when my father was eating his dinner. He ate dinner apart from the rest of us, and with a menu dictated by medical research rather than taste. He looked up from his lentil cutlets in mid-chew. "Whummfumlumpf going?"

"Les and I are having pizza with a professor and some students from St. Oscar's College. I'll be back before—"

"Isnumpgumfscar's bunch of religious fanatics?"

"Oh no, you must be thinking of some other place. St. O's — that's what they call it so it doesn't sound so religious and everything, is a really progressive place." This was the kind of thing calculated to appeal to Dad. "No requirements or rules or anything like that. I think John Anderson went there," I said, naming my father's then-favorite politician. The possibility that St. Oscar's might actually be the kind of freewheeling place that conformed to my father's educational theories temporarily placated him. "And they have a pre-med program," I threw in.

Elated By Details

"Wellumsumpformumpl okay."

"Drive carefully, darling," said my mother, who had been listening to the exchange, but whose intuition told her that St. Oscar's was not really a progressive establishment. "And don't join any cults or anything."

The pizza party was attended by half a dozen students, including a sophomore girl who sat just across the table from me. But to say "just across the table" gives no sense of the gulf between us. She was also on the other side of childhood from me, and she knew it. She spoke of Clapham being one of her favorite "profs," using that unspeakably grown-up contraction just to rub it in.

Her name was Demeter Anacopulous. She had frizzy black hair, dark eyes, and bad skin — perfection itself. Her arms were folded across her orange sweater in a manner that pushed up her breasts, which were also perfect, because they existed.

As an aperitif, Professor Clapham led us through Aquinas' proof of the existence of God: the one that takes you inexorably to the 'uncaused cause' or the 'unmoved mover.'

Les and I tried to outflank him with high school debating tactics. "Okay, so if there is a God," said Les, "then you're saying He caused the Holocaust?"

"Ah ha," said the professor, "now you're talking about the *nature* of God. Is He kind, or cruel or just? Does that mean we're all agreed on the *existence* of God?"

Les and I tried to demur. "There doesn't have to be an

unmoved mover," I said. "Why isn't it just gravity that moves everything?"

"But gravity itself is a phenomenon," said Professor Clapham. "What moves gravity?"

"Physical forces," I said with as much authority as possible.

"That's a nice phrase, but what does it mean? You can't answer real questions with made-up phrases. Or don't you want to get your hands dirty in the details?" Professor Clapham asked with a smirk.

The table was silent; Demeter looked on. "Details? I'm elated by details," I said, extracting a much-needed laugh out of Les. This broke the tension of the debate, but also forced me to explain the faux palindrome technique, which suddenly seemed trivial. In any event, our discussion of God had gone to the dogs, and I didn't even get to use that one.

We tucked into the pizza while Clapham quizzed us about our college choices. I told him I was thinking of going "back east" (as we Midwesterners inexplicably said) for college. The professor thought it was madness to choose one's college on the basis of geography.

"Don't get me wrong," said Clapham, "I've got nothing against New England; I'm from Massachusetts myself. I still go to Menemsha for my summers. Do you chaps know Menemsha?"

"I got amnesia in Menemsha," I said. Demeter laughed at this, and I felt the first stirrings of manhood within me.

"Now cut that out," Clapham said good-naturedly.

Elated By Details

"There's no need for you to go across the country for college. You'd get a first-class education at St. O's."

Toward the end of the evening I fell into conversation with Demeter. Our ages were not so far apart — she was young for a college sophomore, and I was old for a high school senior. We both liked Duran Duran. She had no boyfriend. Fate's long fingers had brought us together. Just before I left, she wrote out her address on a slightly used napkin.

Clapham walked us back to the car. It was an unseasonably cold night in Chicago. "Even the prostitutes are staying inside," observed the professor, as if to prove he could converse with us on "adult" topics.

"It must be a whore frost," I said.

"That's the thing, Blankenship!" Clapham suddenly exclaimed. "You're too glib for your own good. And *you're* not far behind, Calley," he added with a nod to Les. "If either of you goes to one of those fancy East Coast colleges, you'll just get worse. You'll be all patina and no substance! For heaven's sake, let me teach you how to think. Why don't you come and visit the campus some weekend?"

"Oh, I don't know, professor," said Les. "It's debate season and everything." I nodded in agreement, but suddenly thought of Demeter.

"Well, why not?" I said. "I could come up some weekend when there's no debate tournament."

"Splendid. Just call when you have a weekend in mind."

Adam Freedman

* * *

I dashed off a letter to Demeter, telling her of Clapham's invitation. Her reply, which enthusiastically suggested we "hang out" together, convinced me the invitation had to be accepted at all costs.

The next challenge was to convince my parents to let me go up to St. Oscar's, which entailed taking the Amtrak to Milwaukee and then a bus to the college town of Vernon. My father renewed his objection that St. Oscar's was a place of religious fanatics. He waved around a medical journal, rolled up in a threatening manner, lamenting his son's desire to go to a religious commune.

"You can't — you can't possibly be serious. That is one of those places where they teach creationism! There's more science in this one journal than in the whole of St. Oscar's!"

"What's your basis for saying that?"

"Don't use your debating tactics on me!"

"But Professor Clapham says—"

"You can't base your college choice on one professor," my father said. "You have to go to a college where you'll have maximum freedom. I want you to have all the freedom my generation didn't have — freedom to explore yourself intellectually, spiritually, sexually," the last said with a slight hush. "I did not raise a secular humanist Jew to go study with a bunch of Bible-thumpers!" He unfolded his medical journal and started reading. And then, without looking up, added "You'd just end up rebelling later in life."

Elated By Details

After some more lobbying, my father said he would reconsider, after he had a chance to peruse St. Oscar's "literature." I pulled a St. Oscar's brochure from the Guidance Office. It described St. Oscar's as "a secular college in a Christian tradition," and emphasized the college's "back to basics" curriculum and strict morality. That wouldn't do at all.

If only I could explain that I had no intention of actually applying to St. Oscar's! That this whole trip was an excuse to see Demeter Anacopulous. That all I wanted to do was have a look around, sneak into Demeter's dorm room, lose my virginity, go back to Chicago, and announce, on second thought, I'd be applying to Dartmouth instead.

I had to create a phony brochure, which wasn't so easy in those days before personal computers and desktop publishing. I made a photocopy of the real brochure, from which I cut out the college logo. Next, I went to an art supply shop and bought some Letraset stencil letters with which I painstakingly composed a text exulting St. Oscar's "self-directed studies," "coed-housing," the "diversity" of its student body and even it's "Jewish programs." I then had this copied onto colored paper, using a bad photocopier, thus pretty much reproducing the look of a low-budget college brochure, circa 1983.

My father was reasonably pleased by what he read, until he got to the end. "What the devil is this?" he said incredulously. "We're especially proud of our Jewish pogroms? Pogroms! Right there in black and white."

"That's a typo," I said. "I mean, I assume it's a typo. I

think it's 'Jewish programs.' Professor Clapham told me they had special *programs* to make Jewish students more welcome."

"Well, I suppose their heart is in the right place. But it's a pretty insensitive typo."

My father finally relented, but with one fatal twist — that he accompany me to St. Oscar's. My father confessed that his own father had refused to accompany him on his college visits and — in the language then made fashionable by Phil Donahue — he was not about to let the "abused" become the "abuser."

"So I'm going to take my big boy up to college," he said with a cock-eyed smile, in what passed, for him, as a frenzy of emotion. I prepared to die a thousand deaths.

* * *

The trip up to Wisconsin was uneventful, although I couldn't keep my father from getting into the beer. We had gone to the buffet car of the Amtrak in search of lunch. Dad, who insisted on sweating despite the chilly autumn weather, suggested we share a "pint" — he was from Britain, via Canada, evacuated as a child during the war.

"Do you have any beer on draught?" he asked.

"Cans only."

"Right. I guess that'll be two Old Styles then. How about it, Josh? Nothing like a beer on the way up to coll's, eh?"

"I guess."

Elated By Details

We feasted on Amtrak chicken sandwiches, washed down by Old Style and gently agitated by the train and subsequent bus. By the time we arrived at the Vernon Holiday Inn, I was tired, crapulent and mildly nauseous. It was in that state my father and I went to visit the Admissions Office. A student volunteer named Chad gave us a quick tour of the campus — quick because St. Oscar's was tiny, a scattering of small red-brick buildings joined up by flagstone paths.

"Where are the laboratories?" my father demanded, putting the stress on the second syllable in the manner of a central casting Mad Scientist.

"That's the science building over there," said Chad, pointing to a small Georgian house. "Well, science on the first floor, the English Department's upstairs."

My father frowned. "Do you have Jewish pogroms here?"

Chad shrugged his shoulders. "I guess so. We're open to all faiths now."

My father's suspicions were raised. "Are your dorms really coed?"

"Hey Chad, you know what?" I said. Chad looked vaguely alarmed at my new tone of voice. "Professor Clapham said I could sit in on his four o'clock philosophy course. Where would I find that?"

"That would be Rosary Hall. Classroom two."

"*Rosary* Hall?" said my father.

"Great. So Dad, I guess I'll meet you back at the

Holiday Inn?"

"I think, if it's not asking too much, I'd like to join you in this so-called philosophy course."

"Sure," I said. "I guess."

* * *

"Ah, splendid, splendid," cried Professor Clapham when we entered the lecture hall. "Ladies and gentlemen, we are being visited by a prospective student, Josh Blankenship and — oh, you must be Dr. Blankenship! How fortunate to have a physician with us. We're discussing St. Thomas' reinterpretation of Aristotelian Ethics in a Christian context. Of course, in those days, the line between a physician and a meta-physician was much closer than it is perceived to be today. Perhaps you'd like to contribute?"

"Load of rubbish!" my father said in a stage whisper, one hand over his mouth. And then, looking up, he said in an unnaturally chipper voice. "Thanks, I'll just be listening today."

After class, my father announced that he was going back to the hotel, so as to allow Clapham and me time for dinner and a chat.

"I'll see you at breakfast," I said, already counting the hours until my rendezvous with Demeter.

"I have an idea," said Dad. "Why don't you come by my room when you get back, and we'll stop by the hotel bar for a night cap?" My father was turning into something of a wino, which concerned me since that sort of thing often has a Ripple effect.

I had no choice but to agree, knowing I would have to work fast with Demeter. My father wandered off in the direction of the hotel, while Clapham led me across the campus. I soon forgot about my father and started to feel a little of the old self again.

"Bristling under the parental yoke?" said Clapham.

"Only when the yolk ends up on my face."

"Hmmm."

"Does that sound hard-boiled?"

Clapham took me to an early dinner at the cafeteria, and then invited me to his house for sherry. Clapham lived alone in a comfortable campus house, the walls of which were adorned with books and posters from art exhibitions he couldn't possibly have attended. Magritte at the Helsinki Museum of Fine Arts? Where did people get posters like that? As the sun set over the campus, Clapham poured us rather generous portions of the fortified wine.

"I hope you like Amontillado."

"Amontillado is for armadillos."

"Good heavens, you exhaust me. Just sit down. Did you enjoy the lecture?"

"Yes," I said, truthfully. Just as he had at my high school, Clapham had kept the classroom alive by probing students with ever more exacting questions. "It was cool, the way you use the Socratic method, and everything."

"Are you a follower of Socrates?"

"Yes," I said, untruthfully, for at that time I was still using words like "platonic" and "Socratic" without knowing their antecedents.

"Perhaps you'll play Alcibiades to my Socrates," he said sitting beside me on the sofa.

"Yeah. Sure." I took a big swallow of sherry.

The professor laughed. "And you seem to mix well with the students. You certainly hit it off with Demeter the other week." He looked at me with raised eyebrows.

"It was a pleasure Demeter."

"Oh shut up, Blankenship," he said testily. "It's clear that you have an eye for the fairer sex, and in a year's time you'll have all the freedom you need to indulge your desires. But," and now his voice shifted upward to professorial inquiry, "does that mean you should?"

I involuntarily looked at my watch. I had to get out of there. Demeter had instructed me to get to her dorm before 9 o'clock.

"Well, I guess it depends on how it feels at the time," I said, aping something my father would say.

"Ah, the old trap of 'if it feels good, do it.' But there is something special, sacred, about lying with the opposite sex, don't you agree?"

"I thought everyone lied to the opposite sex."

"Stop intentionally misunderstanding me! You have to learn to think about these things — whether you come to this college or some other place."

"Isn't that what religion's all about?" I asked.

Elated By Details

"No. What I'm talking about is a matter of pure logic; however, the truths of religion do not contradict those of logic. In any event, I get the impression that you don't get much religion of any sort in your home."

"Religion? It's the opiate of tapioca."

"Now pay attention. You remember our discussion of the existence of God — the nature of cause and effect, of movement and mover? Yes? Splendid. Now, would you not agree that sexual intercourse is a cause that leads to a certain biologically-determined effect, namely reproduction? The perpetuation of the species? Yes? Very good, Blankenship. This is what the Greeks called teleology; understanding the end towards which nature strives. Now, the question is whether we act morally when we frustrate the natural order—"

Clapham went on in that vein, until he had me agreeing that casual sex, especially with birth control devices, was wicked, *contra naturam*, and several other bad things. It was easy enough to agree with him; the professor's logic was inexorable, troubling, and backed up by all kinds of ancient philosophers. But I was also being agreeable to bring the conversation to an end and get to Demeter's room so I could disregard his logic.

Clapham slid closer to me on the sofa. "I'm glad you agree with me. Of course, that raises another problem. You arrive at this tender age bursting with hormones, full of desire. And yet it is a perversion of the natural order to lie with a woman for any purpose other than procreation."

Clapham lowered his voice. "There is another way out of the frustration," he said, running his hand through my hair, "Alcibiades."

I sat bolt upright. "Is that the time? I really must go. Long day, dogged as a tire. Promised my dad—" I ran out of the door into the freezing night. When I returned to Clapham's front door a few seconds later, he was holding out my forgotten overcoat.

"Now, now, Blankenship, here's your coat. There's no need to be awkward — just a little misunderstanding. Even if you don't want to be Alcibiades to my Socrates, we can still be friends. And if you come to St. Oscar's there's a fighting chance you might actually learn who Alcibiades was."

I thanked him for the sherry and turned away, my walk turning into a sprint when I heard his door close behind me. I made it to Demeter's dorm at 8:50; ten minutes before parietal rules would bar my entrance. Demeter got me past the matron, explaining that I was needed to fix her typewriter, so she could finish her term paper.

She lived in a small double room, decorated with rock star posters and various stuffed animals. Upon my arrival, Demeter's roommate, a fat girl named Carol, snapped her book shut and said, "I guess I'll go down to the Buttery." As she closed the door behind her, I muttered "or the gym." Demeter padded around the room, wearing yellow sweat pants, button-down shirt, and slippers sporting a Minnie Mouse head on each foot.

Maybe it was her get-up that knocked the stuffing out of

me. Maybe it was the fact that Clapham had just hit on me. Or maybe, and this is where I wish I hadn't started this damn thing in the first person, maybe I was finding it unexpectedly frightening to be alone with a girl. I'd made out with girls before, but things had never gone beyond the kissing stage. What was one supposed to do with a girl who was positively willing? I knew clothes were supposed to come off and there was supposed to be a good deal of moaning and groaning. That much was easy. The devil was in the details. I was not elated by those details.

"You seem nervous," said Demeter.

"My father's here."

"I had no idea," she said, and went through a little shtick of looking under the bed, in the drawers, and various other places where my father might be hiding.

"Aw, cut it out," I said. "You know what I mean."

Demeter boiled water in an electric kettle and made us cups of instant cocoa. She told me about her strict Greek Orthodox parents — the way they drummed morality into her. It was making her rebellious. "Do you get all that morality stuff from your parents?"

"No."

"You're lucky."

As Demeter leaned over to pour the water, I caught a glimpse of her cleavage. A pulse of desire challenged my nerves. She produced a bottle of peppermint schnapps from the closet and topped up our cups. The resulting mixture tasted surprisingly like instant cocoa with peppermint schnapps in it. We drank it down while sitting on her bed, and then we drank some more schnapps neat. Demeter was now facing me on the bed, our bodies twisted at three-quarters to each other. It was only then that I noticed how shiny her lip-gloss was.

"Carol will be coming back soon," she said, leaning just slightly closer to me.

"Oh," I said. Taking the hint, I fell into kissing her. We kissed for several minutes, as the forces in my soul did battle — my adolescent desires, the intimidating mystery of a girl's body, and the fear I might, as Clapham had warned, be doing something wicked. Demeter took my hand and placed it on her breast, giving a little sigh of pleasure.

That's when I got scared. "Are you sure this is right?" I said. "I mean, maybe your parents are on to something with all their morality. And what about Professor Clapham. Isn't he your favorite prof? What about Aristotle, and Aquinas, and ethics and all that stuff?" I was not at my most articulate.

"Of course, there's something to it," said Demeter. "I don't disagree with my parents' morality *per se*," she said. "But what they don't know won't hurt them." She threw her arms around my neck and we kissed again.

I extricated myself. "But if their morality is right," I said. "Then isn't this — I mean, what we're doing, isn't it inconsistent?"

She tapped her chin with a finger. "Emerson said 'a foolish consistency is the hobgoblin of little minds,'" she smiled triumphantly, having remembered the quotation.

Elated By Details

"The hobgoblin of little minds! What do you say to that?"

Now was my chance: I could jettison the pretentious moral talk and get down to business. I could take up this invitation, presented on a silver platter with watercress around the edges, to join the adult world of covetousness and moral compromise. It was either that, or just remain a confused smart-alecky high school kid. Demeter looked at me expectantly.

"Hobgoblins are rare in Hoboken," I said, and reached for my coat.

ABROAD AT CHRISTMAS

One thing Jenny Younger could not abide was people who put their Christmas decorations up too early. That was why she was having lunch at the Club Británico, even though she wasn't British. When she first arrived in the country, she had dutifully joined the Club Americano. But then her compatriots had to go and squander their portion of Christmas cheer by stringing the lights up right after Thanksgiving. Jenny switched to the Club Británico and became an expatriate from her own expatriate community.

Today, December 10, Jenny stopped by the club for lunch. She sat at the communal table with the old-timers and ordered the chicken curry. Jenny wanted a touch of the old "mad dogs and Englishman" spirit to fortify her during the hot season. December was high summer in Plata, the

Elated By Details

sultry little republic where Jenny found herself, wedged between Argentina and Brazil.

An older woman in a floppy hat turned to Jenny. "Are you going to the Christmas party?" she said. "You'll want a bit of company this time of year."

This would be her first Christmas abroad. Jenny had promised herself a solid year in Plata before setting foot again in the United States. The first few months had been painless, exciting even. But now — she knew Christmas was going to be hard, the old-timers had told her so. What Jenny didn't tell the old-timers was that she actually took a certain masochistic relish in the loneliness of the holidays.

Just then, Jenny noticed they were putting up Christmas lights in the dining room. Now that was what Jenny called good timing. She turned to the woman in the hat. "I wouldn't miss the party for the world."

The rest of the lunch was devoted to discussing the weather, a topic that distracted most expats from Plata's oppressive politics. The same conversation kept going round and round until Jenny was desperate to talk about anything else, even sports. The woman in the hat asked Jenny how she was holding up in this heat. Jenny smiled maniacally and said: "At least it's a wet heat! If there's anything I can't stand it's a dry heat!" The woman in the hat decided Jenny was a bit peculiar.

If Jenny's new life in Plata fell short of the exotic image she used to have of South America, it was still preferable to living in the U.S. The problem with the U.S. was that it contained one Carl Stern, and that was one too many. He was the reason Jenny was down in that sweltering country, recovering from a divorce that, if nothing else, had left two lawyers very satisfied.

The first of Carl's many crimes was that he had been such a phenomenal kisser. Not just a "good" kisser but a to-die-for kisser. He always knew the right amount of pressure to apply, or when a little playful biting was called for. When he kissed her, as they say, she stayed kissed.

It was probably Carl's perfect kissing that made Jenny ignore all the warning signs. She was aware, for example, that Carl was a bastard — of the Chivalrous Bastard variety. The kind of guy who could make you cry and then offer you a lavender-scented hankie to dry your tears. He also happened to be a charismatic professor with a reputation for sleeping with his students.

"He's a womanizer," said Stacy, who worked with Jenny. They both taught at the journalism school, which was just across campus from Carl's department.

"I've always wondered about that word," said Jenny. "If legalize means to make something legal, and crystallize means to make something crystal, then 'to womanize' must mean to make something into a woman. A womanizer sounds like some kind of household gadget you would use to whip up a few extra women."

Jenny tried to picture the advertisements for the womanizer: *Ladies, do you find yourself short on female dinner guests? Need a fourth for bridge? Try the new womanizer!*

Elated By Details

Or she imagined it as the focus of a sitcom plot: *Frank, have you been using my womanizer again? But Agnes, I thought it was the microwave!*

Jenny had assumed the womanizing would stop when they were married and living in bohemian splendor on the north side of Chicago. But it didn't stop and Carl continued to be, as Jenny secretly called him, the Rake of Wrigleyville. When Jenny finally found proof of his infidelity — a motel receipt — they had a ferocious argument and she came close to leaving him right then, which would, of course, have been the right thing. But he apologized so abjectly, and kissed her so sweetly, she forgave him, sort of.

A schizophrenic cycle of betrayal and passion played itself out over the next few years. Jenny descended into a mild version of raving lunacy, during which she would wander around the empty house at night muttering: "Good kisser, huh? I'll pop him one right in the kisser!" Eventually, she took matters into her own hands, hired a lawyer, and hit Carl with divorce papers. And when she hit him, he stayed hit.

And now, because Carl had been such a good kisser, Jenny was learning just how hot 35 degrees Celsius was. There was something absurdly right about how wrong it felt to be sweating during Christmas. Here in the Southern Hemisphere, the seasons were reversed, the stars were different, and even the water ran down the drain backwards. "There," Jenny would say to herself. "You see? My world has been turned upside down."

Nobody in Chicago had expected Jenny to take a job overseas, but the general idea was fixed in Jenny's mind even before the divorce papers were served. To get away, to escape the glare of all those people she knew from dinner parties and faculty functions. All those people had gone along with the fantasy of Carl and Jenny's happy marriage and were, therefore, complicit in Carl's crimes. Nor did she want to see Michigan Avenue, or Lake Shore Drive, or Cape Cod, or any of the other places that reminded her of Carl. Even the state of Florida was off-limits, for it would remind her that one of Carl's affairs had been with a woman from Florida. She wanted a place that would remind her of nothing.

"I'm moving to South America," she told Stacy one day at lunch. "I have a job with a magazine."

"Don't go!" cried Stacy. And then, when she calmed down a bit, conceded, "I guess being a foreign correspondent *is* more exciting than just teaching journalism. What's the magazine called?"

"*Latin Affairs*," said Jenny. "And that's exactly what I plan to have."

"Wow," said Stacey. "A beautiful divorcee in Latin America. Sounds like the plot of a trashy novel."

"I know. I can't wait to be a broad."

* * *

Elated By Details

When Jenny came back from lunch, she announced that the staff of *Latin Affairs* could finally put up their Christmas decorations. "Christmas" was the word she used, not "holiday." Practically everyone in Plata was Catholic and so she figured "Christmas" was a safe bet. It was funny. After all those years of interfaith marriage and teaching diverse groups of students, she could finally just say Christmas, period. It made her slightly giddy.

The Christmas decoration announcement was one of the few executive decisions Jenny had to make, although her job as "Executive Editor" suggested many such decisions. In reality, most of the magazine's activity consisted of translating Latin American wire services for the benefit of expatriate businessmen. Jenny wrote a little editorial at the front of each week's issue, supervised the translators, and assigned a few local stories.

The magazine had its offices just off of the Avenida Independencia, a wide boulevard indecisively lined with pine trees and palm trees. It was an elegant old building with wooden ceiling fans and French windows that looked out toward the river. When she wasn't staring out those French windows, Jenny spent her time dealing with the translators. They were all native Platense — the adjective for "person or thing from Plata" — and all, save one, were male. The men were chivalrous — of the Latin variety. Although Jenny said very little about her divorce, they naturally assumed she was the wronged party and they doted on her, especially as she struggled with Spanish.

One of the translators, Pablo, went a little further than the others in his flirtation. He had a lean body and wavy black hair. Jenny was tempted, but she thought it was too risky to have an affair with a full-time employee. Jenny did not feel the same reservations about the student intern, Eric, from UCLA. She was admiring him putting up the tinsel when he asked whether she was going home "for the holidays."

"No, Eric, I'm working on being an expatriate."

"No offense or anything, Ms. Younger—"

"Jenny."

"Jenny. But I don't care how long I live outside America, I'll always be a patriot."

He was a cutie all right; the dumb ones always were. And he seemed delighted to fetch Diet Cokes for Jenny. And he had recently stopped displaying the photo of his college sweetheart. *And* he got all huffy whenever Pablo was overly attentive to Jenny.

"It's beginning to look a lot like Christmas," Jenny hummed to herself.

Jenny had had one man since she arrived in Plata. Gustavo was younger than Jenny, but was already a local magnate — he had inherited a shipping business when his father died. He had been sitting to Jenny's left at a Chamber of Commerce luncheon and, since the man on her right spoke no English, they struck up a conversation.

Gustavo had offered to show Jenny various sights, but she had already seen them all. "Well, I suppose we don't

Elated By Details

have very many sights, after all," Gustavo said over coffee. "But have you danced the tango, eh?"

"No. But I would like to learn."

"Then I invite you for a tango lesson!" Gustavo said, delighted. "No funny business, eh? This will be in a café, with lots of people around, nothing to worry about."

Jenny hadn't been worried by the placid-looking Gustavo, who looked to be the most unlikely of tango dancers. But Gustavo turned out to be one of those men who metamorphose on the dance floor, the way some people change behind the wheel of a car. He was tense and masterful — and chivalrous in the right ways.

"It is impossible to dance properly if I do not hold you close," he said with a little smile as he drew her toward him. She developed a whole new appreciation of those bedroom eyes and that sensuous mouth.

After they began sleeping together, Gustavo beseeched Jenny to meet his mother, Violeta. Jenny went, wanting to please Gustavo but also full of misgivings that she was leading the poor boy on. It had been a stifling Sunday afternoon when she went for tea. Cowering before the austere old widow, Pablo became, yet again, quite a different person. Jenny sat through a long and incomprehensible conversation between Gustavo and his mother, which seemed to involve a great deal of apologizing on Gustavo's part. The maid brought in a silver tea service. Gustavo poured the tea while Violeta observed Jenny as though sizing up a potential daughter in law.

"It is so nice to meet you, Jenny," said Violeta, except, with her accent, "Jenny" became "Henny" and "you" became "jew." Jenny had to suppress a laugh.

"So Henny, how are jew?"

"No I'm not, but I used to be married to one."

After a moment of confused silence, Jenny added, "It's just a joke."

"*No importa, mama*," said Gustavo, shooting a dirty look in Jenny's direction. "It doesn't matter."

After that day, Jenny tried to cool things down a little between herself and Gustavo, although they hadn't broken things off. If nothing else, Jenny needed a date for the Christmas party at the Club Británico.

When Eric finished with the Christmas decorations, Jenny asked, "Are you going back to L.A. for Christmas?"

"No. I can't stand my mother's new boyfriend. And my dad, he's just out there, you know?"

No, Jenny did not know. Nor did she know how somebody could profess to be interested in journalism while being so imprecise with his language, but she nodded her head in agreement, because Eric was going to be in Plata for the Holidays.

"Why don't you come to the Christmas party at the Club Británico?" she suggested.

"Sure," he said. "That would be cool. Do I have to wear a tie?"

"Oh yes," said Jenny. "It's beginning to look a lot like Christmas," she hummed.

Elated By Details

* * *

The Club Británico was dressed for Christmas with a kind of sad-clown nostalgia and a collection of hard-core expatriates. Jenny had been surprised to learn most of the members were not British. The club had been built in the days when British investors ran the local economy and, by tradition, it welcomed anyone who could afford the dues. Nowadays, the membership tended toward second-rate businessmen and misfits from various lands.

The club premises were tastefully subdued, except for the air conditioners, which were on full-blast. Frida, the club secretary, who was as British as somebody with one British grandparent could be, greeted each guest with a booming "Happy Christmas!"

A large Christmas tree sat in the corner of the dining room. At the center of each table were a few sprigs of artificial holly surrounding a diminutive British flag. Each place setting included a Christmas cracker, a foil-wrapped tube that looked like an oversized firecracker. Jenny sat at one of the tables, guiding Gustavo and Eric to sit on either side of her. The other places at the table were taken by a bored Frenchman named Tomás, his girlfriend, Justine, and his friend, Phillip, a young American executive with a soup company.

Alec, an older Englishman whose family had been in Plata since before the coup, presided over the table, along with his wife, Doreen. Alec showed everyone how to break open the Christmas crackers by means of little tugs-of-war between dinner companions. Plastic toys and paper hats tumbled out of the crackers. Alec put a hat on his head.

"Now," said Alec, "let's see if we can organize some champagne." He motioned to a waiter.

"What a good idea," said Jenny, who sat across from Alec and who recognized an ally when she saw one.

"Only the English would speak of 'organizing' champagne," said Tomás.

"Mind where you are," said Doreen.

"Tomás hasn't gotten over Waterloo," said Phillip. "He's trying to infiltrate Britain's defenses through the Club Británico."

"Then good luck to him!" said Alec, as the waiter popped the champagne cork. "Let's drink to Tomás!"

Tomás looked embarrassed, but accepted his glass in good cheer.

Eric hesitated. "I don't usually drink this stuff."

"Live a little," Jenny ordered. She couldn't stand Puritanism, especially in the young.

A waiter came around with prearranged plates of roast beef, potatoes, and Brussels sprouts. Another waiter poured everyone a glass of red wine, which Eric didn't usually drink, either. Jenny was more than a little amused to watch him as the wine took effect.

"The thing about Plata?" said Eric, as he downed another glass of local cabernet. "It's all the extremes, you know? The way there are really rich people and really poor people

Elated By Details

and, like, nothing in between?"

"If I may interrupt," said Gustavo, leaning into Jenny's space.

"I mean, I know we have poor people in America, but we also have this middle class—"

Gustavo cleared his throat. "If I may offer a opinion on the subject?"

"Hey," said Eric, putting up his hands in surrender, "it's a free country."

"Actually, it's a military dictatorship," said Jenny

Gustavo was furious, Eric confused, Phillip erupted in laughter. He raised his glass: "To the junta!"

"Mustn't make too many jokes about *that*," said Alec, his blue eyes twinkling. "But I suppose one toast won't hurt."

They drank. The table was beginning to get rather jolly, drinking toasts to Napoleon and Wellington and Simon Bolivar and Liberace. At 11 o'clock, however, *very* early by Platense standards, the waiter announced that the club had run out of wine and champagne.

"Oh well," said Gustavo, "I guess we'd better—"

"What about that punch they were serving before dinner?" said Jenny.

"There's a girl!" said Alec. "I'll just see if I can locate the punch bowl." A few minutes later, Alec returned with the bowl.

"I don't much care for this punch," said Gustavo.

As for Eric, he didn't usually drink rum punch, but he was starting to enjoy breaking all his taboos. "So Jenny," he said, "do you work out? Because you're in, like, really good shape?"

Jenny was mentally rehearsing lines to use on Gustavo: "I'm sorry, I think something I ate disagreed with me," or "I have to be up really early tomorrow," or "Eric's so drunk, I think I better walk him home." And put him to bed.

But even as Jenny's mind was wandering, Eric was growing quiet and morose. Gustavo was talking to Jenny with sharp gesticulations. "This punch is disgusting. Why do we not stop by the café for an espresso or a little oporto?"

"Because I don't want to."

"Excuse me," said Eric, who got up and stumbled to the men's room.

"The first casualty of the evening," said Phillip.

"You'd better make sure he's all right," said Doreen to Alec, after Eric had been away for too long. When Alec returned from the men's room, he announced, with a look of distaste: "Afraid he's got the dry heaves."

Just my luck, thought Jenny. "Oh well," she said brightly. "At least it's a dry heave. If there's anything I can't stand it's a wet heave."

Again, Phillip laughed at her joke. Jenny was beginning to like him; Phillip, with his single-but-looking eyes. She was suddenly self-conscious about whether she looked as drunk as she felt. She straightened her posture and wondered about her hair.

"Jenny, *por favor*!"

"Relax, Gustavo. I'm going to finish my punch with

Elated By Details

these nice people."

Gustavo frowned. "I will smoke a cigarette in the bar. When I come back I would like to leave."

"I don't think he's very happy," said Phillip, after Gustavo was gone.

"No, and I'm a little worried that I enjoy mistreating him."

"Why?"

Jenny folded her arms. "Oh, you know, the usual reasons. Some feminine desire for autonomy, or to exert control. It's hard to explain. Besides, you wouldn't understand, you're just another one of those darn men."

Phillip nodded. "Fed up with the whole phallocracry thing?"

"Well exactly! But I wonder if I've gone too far in—"

"Taking the reins?"

"Yeah. When I take the reins, it pours."

"I wouldn't worry too much about Gustavo," said Phillip. "I've dealt with him in business and he seems like a big boy to me."

"That's what he seems like to me, too."

Jenny asked Phillip why he had moved to Plata, vaguely aware that she did so in the hope the conversation would then swing around to *her* reasons for leaving the States. It was important to have some excuse to mention the divorce so she could measure Phillip's reaction.

"I came for the skiing," said Phillip.

"There are no mountains here," said Jenny.

"I was misinformed."

Jenny laughed. "That's from Casablanca," Phillip added, which she knew, but wished he hadn't said.

Gustavo came back into the dining room. His cigarette was only half-smoked. "Excuse me, Phillip," he said, "I would like to speak to Jenny."

Jenny followed Gustavo out of the dining room. When they were in the foyer, Gustavo cleared his throat and said, "Okay, just one thing I would like to know: what is going on with you tonight?"

"Nothing. I'm just trying to have a good time."

"If you intended to ignore me, why did you invite me tonight?"

"I'm not ignoring you. It's just that I'm having a good time and you're not. I'm sorry, but I can't help that."

"Of course you can," said Gustavo. "You could have told me you were going to invite that stupid child, Eric, to the table, and that you were going to flirt with him the whole evening."

"I'm sorry if I bruised your ego."

He threw up his hands. "Why are you behaving like a bitch?"

"I am not a bitch," she said slowly, with emphasis. A bitch is what everybody thought she was when she was Carl's wife, but that was not her nature. People so often failed to distinguish between women who are bitches by nature, and those who just go through bitchy phases. Jenny had just been going through a phase; one that ended when she cast aside her married name and became, once again,

Elated By Details

fun-loving Jenny Younger. When people at the university used to comment on her hardness, she would tell them, "I'm only Stern by marriage."

"Well, then you're being irresponsible," said Gustavo. "You've been in this country for five months! What do you know? I have a reputation. My company ships products for Tomás' family, and for Alec's company, and for Phillip's company, too."

"Oh, Phillip's fine," said Jenny.

"That's not the point. It's not nice to be humiliated in front of people you have to do business with. The way you flirted with that boy! And making jokes about the junta! That's fine for you, but I don't have the luxury of running back to Chicago when I get bored with Plata."

"Gustavo, everybody is drunk. Nobody will remember a thing." Jenny was not enjoying this.

"That is not the point!" Gustavo shook his head. "Let's go. I will drop you off at your apartment."

"I'll take a taxi."

"Fine. You really should stop behaving like a child," he said, and started to walk away.

"Give my regards to your mother!" she yelled after him.

Jenny went into the ladies' room, kicked the trashcan, stubbed her toe, and hopped around on one foot.

"Shit, shit, shit, shit, shit!"

When that was over, she composed herself and made her way back to the table. Phillip was nursing a glass of punch with no serious intention of drinking it.

"Where is everybody?" said Jenny.

"Tomás and Justine left, and Alec and Doreen are taking Eric home. Alec said he might be back, but I doubt it."

"So it's just us." Okay, she thought: I am ready to give up the tough broad routine. I am *so* ready to give up the tough broad routine. Ask me out, Phillip. Take me home, Phillip. There's a good boy.

Phillip smiled. "How's the old control-and-revenge game?"

"It's not going totally according to plan. But thanks for asking."

"Let me help you," said Phillip, reaching into his wallet. "Here's my card. I won't ask for your number, even though I'd like to see you. Whether or not we ever speak again is totally in your control. Rest assured, I'll be waiting by the phone like a schoolgirl."

* * *

It was not clear to Jenny that calling Phillip would be a victory in the control game. You probably had more control when you were being pursued than the reverse. She was also slightly concerned that Phillip's happy relinquishing of the initiative might be some sort of weird submissive thing. In any event, the question was academic over the weekend, since she only had Phillip's work number.

On Monday, she thought about calling Phillip, but was distracted by the arrival of a vast bouquet of roses. They

Elated By Details

were from Gustavo, with a sweet little note, signed with a kiss. Gustavo came to pick her up after work, looking dapper and contrite.

"You must forgive me," he said. "I lost my temper."

"You had every right to," said Jenny, and she meant it.

"I invite you for a walk, and then maybe a little dinner, eh?"

"I'd like that."

They walked down the promenade that ran along the river. Shops were shuttering their windows and the cafes were coming to life. Gypsy women crisscrossed the promenade selling flowers. Jenny was getting to like the rhythms of the place.

Gustavo stopped at the balustrade and turned to her. "Look at how beautiful the moon is," he said.

Jenny thought: who writes your material? "It sure is," she said.

"Jenny, I don't know why I get so angry at you sometimes!"

"It's okay, really."

"I suppose you think I am a child, like Eric. But it's only because I'm so crazy about you. And I think, in reality, you are a little crazy about me, too, no?"

"Sure, Gustavo. A little."

He took her in his arms and kissed her. Jenny responded. After five months in South America, she was just about able to enjoy kissing in public. While Gustavo held her, Jenny thought about how exhausting these men were, and how romantic the city was, and what a good kisser Gustavo was.

"Tomorrow," she said to herself firmly. "Tomorrow I will call Phillip."

THE SMELL OF SUCCESS

I was trying to explain those lugubrious passages at the beginning of Proust's great novel. As usual, I did so by comparing Proust to myself.

I wasn't saying that Proust and I are the same—just that we're comparable. And, by the way, that comparison wasn't even my idea, originally. Better men than I have compared the plays of Gabriel Frond (me) to the novels of Marcel Proust. My work has a similar emphasis on memory, on the restless search for "lost time."

In any event, since we seemed to have gotten on to the subject of my plays, I took the opportunity to say a few words about my dramaturgical technique. I told them anyone who had seen my work — and that would be nobody, since the theatrical establishment has not yet deigned to produce my scripts, but just suppose somebody had seen my plays — would recognize me as a genius.

At that juncture, I thought it appropriate to demonstrate that being a "genius" isn't all beer and skittles, as many people seem to think. With one hand clutching the lapel of my blazer, I looked out the window. Outside, a cold drizzle was falling on a quiet street. "True art," I said, "is as bleak as this weather. If you ask me why I refuse to put dialogue in my plays, my answer is this: what could anybody say about a day like today?" I let the rhetorical question float away, leaving nothing but existential angst in its wake.

I turned away from the window and faced my audience, only then remembering it did not consist, as I had been imagining, of the fellows of the Academy of Arts and Letters, but rather, a 10th grade biology class at P.S. 200. They were not listening. Part of the problem was my status as a substitute teacher, which makes any classroom discussion a risky proposition, at best. The other part of the problem was neatly summarized by one of the pupils: "Excuse me, Mr. Frond," he said, "but, like, what you're saying has totally nothing to do with biology."

For a second or two, I was so taken by the sound of "totally nothing" — a phrase I vowed to work into my own poetry — that I could not even formulate an answer. Besides, the student's point was essentially correct. I had strayed far from the ostensible subject of the class, but I had no intention of teaching biology, a subject about which I know nothing. Such, I'm afraid, is the state of public edu-

Elated By Details

cation in New York City.

"Yeah," a few students began to mumble, "what about biology? How about some biology?" In this way, the little urchins managed to be disruptive while impersonating people who desired to learn.

"Biology is about life," I improvised. "And what is life but the sum of our memories?"

A dead frog came flying from the back of the classroom; I had to duck to avoid it. It landed on my desk and the class erupted in laughter. Not only was the dead frog disgusting to look at, but it positively stank of formaldehyde. The smell of the thing was overwhelming.

One thing you ought to know about me is that I have a large, and very sensitive nose. That dead frog smell reached into my nose and burrowed into my head until the formaldehyde had penetrated my skull. The fumes smelled as though they would attack my brain, pickle it, freeze it, and probably cause irreversible damage to my cognitive function. I repeat: my sense of smell is acute.

The students were waiting for my reaction — almost as though they were hoping for the proverbial iron fist to come down upon them. I looked out at the assembled delinquents and surprised even myself by yelling: "This is no time for Aristophanes!"

That's another thing about me. Sometimes, there's a disconnect between what I mean to say and what I do say. Like just then? What I meant to say was: "who threw that frog?" And then, when the perp had identified himself, I was going to say: "See me after class!" But somewhere in the recesses of my mind, an association was forming — between the dead frog and *The Frogs* — which is, of course, what made me cry Aristophanes. These involuntary utterances stem from the same root as my genius.

Any teacher can tell you the window of opportunity for disciplining a high school class is very small. Unfortunately, I had squandered my opportunity with the Aristophanes crack. As the students made light of my apparent insanity, I fished a day-old *New York Times* out of my leather satchel and used it to cover up the dead frog.

I looked at the clock. There were ten minutes left to go, but I had discretionary authority to dismiss class five minutes early. I made a few half-hearted attempts to restore order — the kind of gestures calculated to eat up some time without really interfering with the chaos reigning in the classroom. It worked perfectly. The students ignored me, turning on portable radios, hacking up dead frogs, and throwing things at one another.

I raised my voice: "I can see there won't be any more learning here today. I'm dismissing class early!"

The students heard this and quickly gathered up their things and started running for the door. The last to leave were a couple of girls, budding Lolitas, who sauntered at their own insolent pace. One of them, a Puerto Rican girl with full, sensuous lips and precocious breasts passed close to me and then nudged her companion in the ribs.

"Mr. Frond is totally checking me out!"

Elated By Details

The girls giggled and threw their arms around each other in one of those displays of Sapphic affection that often possess girls on the cusp of womanhood. As though I would be "checking her out." I stamped my feet at the thought. And then I reached into my satchel and took out the remains of a chocolate bar I had been saving. I stuffed it into my mouth and masticated vigorously.

A male teacher is forever pursued by girls in search of father figures. I could have deflowered a dozen girls by this time, but that would have meant the end of teaching. And teaching was my only source of income; that is, until my play would be produced, for I had finally written *the* play that would establish my reputation!

My teaching gig being over for the day, I headed to the administration office to collect the forms I needed to get paid. The money was not good, but I know of no job with lower expectations than substitute teaching. Provided there are no homicides on your watch, you're a raging success. I breezed into the administration office, the strap of my leather satchel slung across my chest in the manner of a Gen-x hipster.

"Well if it isn't Gabriel!" said Roseanne, a secretary in the administration office. "To what do we owe this unexpected pleasure?"

Roseanne never missed an opportunity to flirt. She had a very pretty face, and was a good 30 or 40 pounds overweight. As I exchanged greetings with various school bureaucrats, I noticed Roseanne gazing at me with this silly look of adulation. A certain sense of decency told me I ought not give this poor thing any hope I might reciprocate her feelings. Such hopes would only be dashed in the end, causing more pain for her.

"Roseanne," I said, "you grow more beautiful every day."

The other secretaries gave hoots and whistles. "Oh Gabriel!" said Roseanne. "How did the biology class go?"

"I wanted to talk about Proust, but the kids today! All they're interested in is Aristophanes."

The look of confusion on Roseanne's face quickly dissolved into a smile. She waved her hand in a playfully dismissive gesture. "Half the time I think you make those words up!"

"You really are bovine," I said.

She looked modestly into her lap, as one who had just been paid a great compliment, and said, "Thanks, Gabe, you're sweet."

This was one of my little games. "I mean it," I said, leaning towards her. "You're the most jejune woman at P.S. 200."

"Shhh, Gabe, you'll make the others jealous!"

She shampooed with Pert, cleaned her teeth with Colgate, and dabbed herself with Obsession. All of these facts, and more, came to me via that incredibly sensitive organ to which I have already alluded, viz., my nose.

"I wanted to arrange for my emoluments," I said.

"Oh, I remember that one!" cried Roseanne. "That means money, doesn't it?"

Elated By Details

"That's right. I've come for a stalk of salary."

I would be lying if I said it wasn't gratifying to have a woman so obviously interested in me. But Roseanne was not bread for my mouth, as the French say. Not that I'm any prize. In addition to the big nose, I have terrible posture, greasy hair, and only one eyebrow — over both eyes, that is. So, I'm not holding out for a beauty queen; all I ask for is a certain intellectual mettle. But I do ask for that.

Roseanne got up and walked to the file cabinet, sashaying her ample hips for my benefit. As she dug up the proper forms for me, she was to be heard repeating "stalk of salary. I got to remember that one. I didn't know salary came in stalks."

"Only when your employer is parsley-monious," I said when she returned.

"Well that certainly describes this school!" said Roseanne, a little huffily. She handed me the reimbursement forms and I scramed, promising to fill them out by the end of the week. I walked to the subway and began the long ride to Brooklyn.

* * *

I was born of progressive parents. My mother was a feminist back in the 1960's, when feminists were still smart enough to let men earn all the money. The economic freedom of that arrangement gave my mother ample time to explore various theories she had about the cultural roots of male domination.

My mother loved me, I believe; but she was also very concerned about the psychosexual bond between a boy and his mother. The male tendency to objectify women: the adulation and the disgust, the virgin-whore complex, and so on, sprang from men's inability to distinguish between women in general and their own mothers. For example, little boys spend their formative years clinging to their mothers, constantly breathing in the scent of their perfume. In later life, the smell of perfume triggers the inevitable, Pavlovian reaction — the man must have that woman, he must have his mommy.

To break that vicious cycle, my mother swore off all perfume. Instead, she slathered herself with a seaweed-based concoction, which, I suppose, was also meant to instill a subconscious ecological bent. As a result, the smell of a woman's perfume, Roseanne's Obsession, for example, does not effect me as it does other men. Granted, I have experienced some strange pangs when visiting the seashore but, living in New York City, one doesn't often smell seaweed.

Another thing my mother did to keep me from "worshipping" her in an unhealthy way was to employ a strategy of thwarted expectations. In my formative years, she made it a point to leave me alone in the apartment for long stretches of the day. Even when she took me to a playground, she would disappear without warning, coming back to find a frightened little boy; traumatized, perhaps, but wiser in ways he couldn't yet perceive. Her *coup de grace*,

Elated By Details

as it were, was her permanent departure from the family in the 1970's. She left for Los Angeles with a man who had ambitions of becoming a director. She has not been heard from since.

My father did not remarry. The responsibilities of single parenthood sat uneasily on his shoulders and he ended up relying largely on the help of his own mother, that is, my grandmother, who lives in the same cramped apartment in Bensonhurst where my father grew up.

Deprived of my mother, all I could think to do was search for that seaweed lotion, the smell of which might bring me solace. I didn't know where to look or whom to ask; kosher delis and hardware stores seemed as plausible as pharmacies to me. And, of course, I had no idea what brand name was involved and so I asked for the stuff in the broadest possible terms. Shopkeepers all over Brooklyn laughed at the funny little boy who claimed to be looking for "seaweed stuff" for his mother.

"Why don't you ask your mother what it's called?" they would ask me, when I failed to provide more particulars.

Granny did her best to help my father raise me; although, when I finally got around to asking her, she refused to help me look for the seaweed lotion. "Better to forget about it," she would say. "No point stirring up a lot of memories." Over time, Granny and I became quite close, especially since my father passed away some years ago. And now, as I trudge through my thirties, one great comfort is the mature relationship I have established with Granny.

Adam Freedman

* * *

I got off the subway in Bensonhurst and walked to the apartment. As usual, Granny had tidied up my bedroom and, knowing how exhausting I find substitute teaching, she had run out to the grocery store to get me some treats. My grandmother tried to make our time together as pleasant as possible. I suppose she knew I would move out as soon as I found a producer for my play.

"Why don't you sit down," said Granny. "I got you some cheese and crackers."

These are the kind of everyday gestures that so often serve to confirm one's faith in humanity. As Granny set the cheese plate before me, I silently reminded myself to show my appreciation for her.

"Where the hell did you get this cheese?" I said. "The Rue Morgue? Or do you have a corpse in here?"

"What?"

"Habeas corpus, Granny?"

"No, it's limburger."

"Never mind," I said, annoyed at myself more than anything. It was that disconnect again.

"While you were out, I tidied your room," Granny said rather primly. "I hope you don't mind."

"Of course not, Granny. Although it is superfluous."

"Oh Gabe, you and your compliments! It was just a little light cleaning." Yes, it was the same game of polysyllabic confusion I played with Roseanne. How else could

Elated By Details

one keep one's sanity?

I spread the cheese on a cracker and stuffed it into my mouth and quickly followed with another. Had I been less constrained by convention, I'd have stuffed a cracker in each ear as well.

Granny poured me a glass of apple juice, which I managed to drink by imagining it was a perfectly chilled glass of Sancerre and my grandmother was a waitress, and I was a completely different person. At length, I noticed Granny was smoothing out her apron and worrying her hair curlers. She wanted to say something.

"Gabriel?"

"Yes Granny?"

"While I was tidying up I couldn't help noticing your play. It was just lying on top of your desk."

"Of course it was lying on top of my desk," I said dryly. "That's the last place the authorities would think to look."

"I didn't disturb it, Gabe. I just sat there at your desk for a little while and read it through. You don't mind do you? I was so curious to see what you've been working on all these months."

I sat down. "Granny, how many times do I have to tell you? The play won't mean anything to you. It's full of irony."

"Oh, I know, but I just skipped over that." Granny sat down across from me. "It's a very nice play, Gabe."

"Thanks," I said, stuffing more cheese and cracker into my mouth.

"There is," said Granny, "just one thing I don't understand. You call the play *Life in an Ol'Factory Town* but I didn't see anything about a factory in there."

"Of course not! The title is a play on words, Granny. It's not about an 'old factory' town; it's about an 'olfactory' town, a mythical town in which everything — the economy, communications, transportation — is based on the sense of smell. Olfactory, get it? That's what I mean about irony. It's not about factories at all, except to the extent that it is a requiem for the post-industrial West."

"I like stories about the Old West."

"It's not — Oh, never mind."

I took a swig of the perfectly chilled Sancerre and started looking through the stack of mail on the table, hoping Granny would take the hint. No dice.

"Gabe? How come nobody says anything in your play?"

"Dialogue is death to drama," I began to say, and then thought better of it. The fact is, dialogue's a crutch all too many playwrights lean on, and it simply was not appropriate to the subject matter. My play was about smell and memory; the olfactory sense being the least appreciated of the senses. I have 62 pages of stage direction, some interesting set designs, and a plan to distribute scratch-and-sniff cards to the audience, a technique pioneered by filmmaker John Waters.

In the final analysis, what I am trying to do is capture that moment when a man begins the long retreat into his own memory. Is it not when the inevitability of Death final-

Elated By Details

ly sinks in? As we begin to see the shadowy outlines of the Grim Reaper, as we get a whiff of his stale breath, we pack up our thoughts and head into the past. And the past, I assert, is a land of smells: lavender soap; pancakes and syrup, custard pie, freshly-cut grass, burning leaves, hot chocolate. And seaweed.

But just try explaining that to an 80-year-old woman.

"I'm going to add the dialogue later," I said. I stuffed another cracker into my mouth and slipped into a daydream featuring the large Soho loft I would someday purchase with the royalties from my play.

* * *

That evening, I took myself to a book launch hosted by a leading publisher. An old college friend named Howard invited me to the event, which was held in a Chelsea gallery.

Let me be perfectly honest: these parties are awful and are attended by complete philistines. But the food and drink are free and it is the only way to meet somebody who might be able to advance my play. Not for me the life of a "starving artist," whose manuscripts are discovered and celebrated only after his death.

I was drinking red wine from a plastic cup and attacking the raw vegetable platter — an artist gets his roughage where he can — when Howard greeted me. Howard did book reviews for *Art Seen* magazine, which is how he got himself invited to things like this.

"*Sa va?*" said Howard.

"*Vie gehts?*" I said. "Any sign of Darcy?"

I was referring to Darcy Dourmuss, the theater critic for *Art Seen*. Months ago, I had set my sights on Darcy as a possibly sympathetic ally, based on some nice comments she made about a poem I had published in *Subtext* magazine. A poem which, incidentally, earned me nothing more than a year's subscription to *Subtext* — a result that reminded me of the famous pie eating contest, for which the prize was more pie.

Anyway, Darcy struck me as a person who could make things happen in the theater world. After some persistent nagging on my part, Howard agreed to give Darcy a copy of *Life in an Ol'Factory Town*.

"She'll be here any minute," said Howard. "Working on anything new, Gabe?"

"Why should I write anything new? A person is lucky if he writes one masterpiece in his life, and I'm busy polishing *Ol'Factory Town*. In fact I'd like to tell Darcy about a few revisions to the Second Act. It seems to me that the central conflict—" I was slipping into self-absorption, which I tried to remedy by turning the conversational tables on Howard. "What are you working on?"

"Getting laid," he said. "There's this performance artist coming to the party tonight; goes by the name of Pussy Teeth. She's not very attractive—"

"Then you have something in common," I blurted out, and instantly regretted it. Although it was true enough. Even

Elated By Details

compared to me, Howard came up short in the looks department. "Just kidding, Wit," I said, reverting to his old college nickname, Wit being short for Wittgenstein, which was both his last name and his favorite philosopher.

"By the way, Wit, I loved your piece about Hickenlooper's linguistics."

"Thanks. It's funny, so few people realize Hickenlooper is just another Saussurian in the sense of pure language. Hey! Pussy Teeth just walked in. I'd better make my move." Without more, Howard made his way toward somebody wearing black leather pants. She looked to be a woman of easy virtue who probably hopped from bed to bed with various members of the art-critical establishment. Tonight would be Howard's night. I stamped my feet.

* * *

When I finally caught sight of Darcy, I felt that prickly sweat on my back that usually accompanies stress. I gulped down my red wine and immediately got another and drank that too. I watched Darcy as she made small talk with various agents and editors. Her thick black-rimmed glasses, untamed hair, and frumpy "retro" polyester pants suggested a certain determination to cast herself as "biggest extrovert in the room."

The crowd seeped around me, stepping on my shoes and sloshing wine on my blazer. For a second or two, I was disgusted at my own attempts to curry favor with the petty arbiters of taste in Manhattan. I had just about made up my mind to leave the party when Darcy beckoned me toward her. I expected nothing better than the patronizing sarcasm one usually gets from these types.

"Darcy," I said when we were face-to-face, "don't let's spoil that angelic composure of yours by discussing my miserable excuse for a play."

"Don't be silly, Gabriel. I absolutely love your play!"

"Darcy," I skipped a beat. "If this is some cruel joke of yours—"

"It's not a joke, you goof! The play is brilliant — totally subversive and great! I love the whole smelling thing," she said. Speaking of which, I could tell she had eaten Thai food recently, and was using a cucumber-based moisturizer.

"No accolade has ever meant as much to me," I said, choking up slightly.

We gabbed for a while in a spirit of mutual love fest, with her extolling my play, and me her criticism, including her new book of feminist dramatic theory, *Theat-her*. A banker-type was lurking nearby. He turned out to be Darcy's husband, Jonathan.

"Honey," Darcy said to Jonathan, "say hello to Gabriel, who's written a fabulous play."

"'Kind of play?" said Jonathan, who skipped the beginning of sentences, presumably for efficiency's sake.

"Musical," I says, for now my spirits were soaring.

"Musical?" said Darcy.

"I like to think of it as the libretto for John Cage's 'Four

Elated By Details

and Half Minutes of Silence.'"

"Brilliant!" she screamed.

That sort of banter continued for another minute or two, at which time Jonathan began agitating to leave. "'bout that time, huh Darce?"

Darcy assented and was revving up her good-byes. I figured it was now or never to enlist her help. "So," I said, "what do you think we can do to get my play into production?"

"Oh, Gabriel, how should I know? I'm just a critic, I don't *produce* plays, for heaven's sake!" She and Jonathan shared a laugh. At me? Having had my self-loathing turned away at the front door, I now found it sneaking in through the back door.

"But you must know people—" I stammered, "you know, people who can help me." I was misting up again.

"Isn't he adorable?" said Darcy to her husband. "Couldn't you just hug him?"

"'Wouldn't go that far."

"Wait! I know what to do!" Darcy cried, punching Jonathan in the arm. "Get Stephen to talk to Sarabeth!" Darcy turned to me: "The senior director at Jon's firm is the father of Sarabeth Lycasin. You know, from *Cuties*?" she said, naming a young starlet and her most recent box office smash.

"I can't imagine somebody like that would be interested in my play," I said.

"Think about it," said Darcy. "Sarabeth is one of those

kids who wants to become a Serious Actress, you know? So she wants to start doing theater in between movies. The problem is, she can't act. She can barely read."

"I get it," I said. "What could be better for her than an avant-garde play with *no dialogue*?" This time I laughed along with Darcy and Jon.

I know, I know. I was supposed to turn my large nose up at the mention of Sarabeth Lycasin. She reeked of crass commercialism; she and her ilk were the enemy of True Art. But if she was good enough for Darcy Dourmuss, she was good enough for me. Besides, I was not averse to a bit of box office success if it got me closer to that million-dollar Soho loft.

"Oh, honey, this is perfect!" Darcy cried, pummeling her husband with both fists. "You have got to get Sarabeth interested in Gabriel's play!"

* * *

The next morning I returned to P.S. 200 for another teaching gig.

It was Heraclitus who observed that change is constant; that you cannot dip your foot in the same river twice because it won't be the same river the second time. Or the same foot, for that matter. That observation applied to me, for this was not the same Gabriel Frond as the day before.

The new Gabriel Frond was a Playwright; his genius having been confirmed by no less a person than Darcy

Elated By Details

Dourmuss. His play was being bandied about as a vehicle for Sarabeth Lycasin. The new Gabriel Frond was wearing a corduroy blazer and a paisley silk scarf. He — I substitute-taught an English class with supreme confidence, dishing out a dozen detentions, half of which were for indignities I had suffered the previous semester.

After class, I breezed into the administration office and appropriated for myself a vacant chair. I plopped down, flung the silk scarf around my neck, and crossed my legs.

"Hello all!"

"Make yourself at home," one of the secretaries said.

Roseanne was there, bending over a filing cabinet. There were blond highlights in her hair, all the better to bring out her rosy cheeks, and her nails had a fresh coat of bright red polish. She was wearing a pink sweater, in the "V" of which her ample breasts jostled for position. She looked up from the filing cabinet and gave me a coquettish wave. "Hi Gabe," she said. "What's new?"

"I'm flush with Heraclitus," I said and it was true enough. Roseanne herself seemed to be subject to the law of constant change, for she appeared uncommonly sexy. Or perhaps I just saw her through different eyes. Either way, I finally understood what it was that had always bothered me about Roseanne: it was the fact that she was just *within* the realm of possibilities for me. Deep down, I always sensed the danger if I ever got involved with Roseanne: I might actually end up marrying her and settling into a some sort of plebian version of Mr. Chipps.

I had a different perspective now that I was in business as an Artist. Roseanne no longer posed any serious threat of marital entanglement. Rather, she merely presented herself as the first of many lovers to whom I could now lay claim, along with NEA grants and screaming fan clubs. She wanted to be had, and by God, I would have her.

I walked over to Roseanne and her filing cabinet. "Got any plans for this weekend?"

By the time I left it was settled: we would meet on Saturday afternoon at the Metropolitan Museum of Art. From there, a drink and, perhaps, dinner. I was excited by the prospect. Keep in mind that I had not had intercourse for over a year. It's a matter of focus: you need total focus when you're writing a masterpiece. Besides, living with one's grandmother is bad news, intercourse-wise.

*　*　*

On Friday, Darcy phoned to let me know that Sarabeth Lycasin was "definitely interested" in the play and wanted to read the latest draft of the script. She gave me Sarabeth's address.

"Get her that play as soon as possible," said Darcy.

I worked through the night on Friday and well into Saturday. Even as the hour of my date with Roseanne drew near, I was still re-working this or that bit of the play. I was not about to take any chances now that success was beckoning me like the very grapes of Tantalus. The time I had

Elated By Details

allotted for napping, showering and shaving found me still at my desk. As they say, it's great to be a writer, but the paperwork is murder.

I was an hour late for my date with Roseanne, but she was still waiting for me at the Met. Unshaven and exhausted, I was also carrying a disk with the latest version of *Life in an Ol'Factory Town*. You see, I don't own a printer and I can't afford to pay the confiscatory prices at those copy shops. Usually, I ask Roseanne to print my plays in the school administration office. Standing on the steps of the Met, I explained the situation to Roseanne. To her credit, she didn't even hesitate. We hopped on a subway and went to P.S. 200 — she has a key — and printed out the play. Afterwards, we took the subway back to Manhattan where we left a copy of the play with the doorman of Sarabeth Lycasin's building.

Roseanne was a trooper through the whole thing, even though we sort of skipped drinks and dinner. The only sour note came at the end, after I had escorted her home. I was kissing her goodnight as we stood outside her apartment.

"Gabriel, that's enough!" She peeled my hands off of her. "Not that it hasn't been a dream date, Gabe," she said, smoothing out her dress. "But a girl does like a little romance. Maybe next time we could even have some dinner?"

I agreed and slouched back to Granny's feeling distinctly unfulfilled. I locked myself in my room and extracted one of the chocolate bars I kept in my desk. I slowly unwrapped the bar and stuffed half of it in my mouth. Thinking of

Roseanne, I furiously masticated.

I had promised Roseanne a second date the following weekend, but I didn't follow up because I had become too preoccupied with Sarabeth Lycasin. My life was in her tiny, semi-literate hands. Did she like my play? Did she understand it? Would she do it? I could not go out on dates; I could not teach; I could not do anything that might take me away from the phone. I forbade my Granny from using the phone — a policy that required constant monitoring and precipitated some furious rows. It didn't matter, if all went according to plan, I would be moving out soon enough.

After three weeks, the call finally came. It was Sarabeth's agent, a high-strung woman named Dixie Von Slivovitz.

"Sarabeth is just in love with your play, Mr. Frond," said Dixie. "She's in love with it! She does have a few questions and concerns. Nothing major. Gabriel, can I call you Gabriel? Great. Anyway, Sarabeth would like to meet you and talk about the project. Is that okay with you? Great. How does Friday work for you?"

After the arrangements were made, I slammed down the phone and screamed "Excelsior!" Then I ran into the kitchen.

Granny was sitting at the table, drinking tea. "Does this mean I can use the phone now?" she said.

"You may have unfettered use of the phone," I said, cinching the belt of the bathrobe I'd been wearing for the past three weeks. I reached into the cupboard and extracted

Elated By Details

Granny's only bottle of booze, some kind of sugary liqueur. I unscrewed the sticky cap and poured myself a tall glass, to Granny's lengthening frown.

"It's three o'clock!"

"My how time flies," I said and gulped down the syrup, which sent a shiver through my body. "By the way, I'm moving out of here."

"With the money you make? You must be drunk already!"

But Granny didn't know that Sarabeth loved my play — loved it, loved it, loved it. Soon enough, a production company would be formed. The first thing they would have to do is buy the script, from Gabriel Frond, and for a lot of money. And then there would be royalties, film rights, television rights, merchandising and tie-ins: a lifetime stream of income from the *Ol'Factory Town*.

I raised my glass. "Proust!" I cried, and drank. Something about Granny's expression must have touched me, because I got another glass from the cupboard and poured her a drink and then topped up my own.

"No hard feelings, Granny. The fact is — and I don't think I'm going out on a limb here. I've been discovered. My play is going to be produced off-Broadway, or maybe even on Broadway. And with a movie star!"

"Gabe, that is good news," she said, but did not pick up her glass.

"Come on Granny," I said, holding mine close to the lips, "here's mud in your eye!"

Granny thawed a bit, and toasted me with her tea. I drank the rest of my glass and then drank what was in hers.

I put on some clothes and spent the rest of the afternoon drinking beer in a local Irish pub. I tried to get Wit to join me, but I couldn't reach him. In the early evening, I made my way, unannounced, to Roseanne's apartment. She invited me in and switched off the TV.

"Have you been drinking?" she asked, after I had tripped over one of her chairs.

"Celebrating," I said, while still splayed out on the floor. She helped me up, and I gave her a brief account of my conversation with Dixie Von Slivovitz.

"Congratulations!" she said. And then she added, rather sweetly, "I guess that means we won't see you around the school any more. I don't think you like the school very much, anyway."

"It isn't the school I hate, it's the Principal of the thing."

"I know what you mean," she said, nodding gravely.

I was feeling reckless. "At times like this," I said, drawing closer to her, "you're perfectly obtuse."

"Flattery will get you everywhere."

We fell into some pretty serious canoodling. My right hand worked its way down from her cheek to her neck, and then to her shoulder. After a minute, I laid my palm on one of her mountainous breasts, and met with no resistance. I moved the hand down and slipped it underneath her blouse. In a few seconds, I would unsnap her bra and watch the treasures come spilling out, like a swollen piñata finally

Elated By Details

bursting. The hand moved into position.

She pushed me away with a force that sent me off the sofa and on to the floor for the second time. "Gabriel! Don't you remember what I said about romance the other night? I mean, I'm happy for your play and all, but still—"

"You want romance?" I said. "How about the Rainbow Room Saturday night?"

"Now that's more like it!"

"It's a date."

Not wanting to spend the last of my money on a taxi, I stumbled to the subway. Along the way, I stopped in a bar where I spent the last of my money on a scotch. The next morning I woke up to a spinning bedroom, thanks to the quantity and variety of booze I'd drunk. I ran to the bathroom and vomited. And then I returned to bed, and waited for Friday.

* * *

I was half an hour early on Friday. Sarabeth's agent, Dixie, had arranged for an artist-to-artist meeting at one of those Parisian-style brasseries on the Upper West Side. The maitre d' showed me to a banquette table. I ordered a vodka-tonic to steady my nerves.

I was almost finished with my second drink when a beautiful blond woman, about college age, approached my table. This was Sarabeth.

"Gabriel?" she said, tilting her head and pronouncing

my name with a short "a," as though I were French.

"That's me!" I said, standing up.

"Hi, I'm Sarabeth Lycasin," she said, and quickly extended her hand in greeting. No cheek kissing for her. "Sorry to keep you waiting." As she said this, she yanked a strand of blond hair and looped it over her ear.

"Think nothing of it. And, if it isn't too impertinent, may I say that you're even lovelier in person than on the screen, Ms. Lycasin."

"Please, call me Sarabeth."

Sarabeth sat on the banquette, while I resumed my seat. She repeated how much she loved my play, and we made some small talk about the "creative process."

I am not the sort of person who normally falls for movie stars. In fact, I had never actually seen any of Sarabeth's films, notwithstanding my comment about her being lovelier in person than on the screen.

And yet, I was immediately filled with these rapturous feelings for her. I could barely contain myself. At first, I assumed I was simply being carried away by the emotion of the moment, what with my head already a bit fuzzy from the cocktails. But as we settled into conversation I realized something was playing havoc with my nose. I could not immediately identify the smell.

Sarabeth suggested we have a quick bite and then go over the play. I ordered a bottle of wine before learning Sarabeth didn't drink — she was barely old enough anyway. Just as well, I thought, hoping a bottle of wine would drown

Elated By Details

my lust for her. It had the opposite effect.

It wasn't for nothing that Sarabeth was a box office draw. She had bright eyes, pouting lips, and a model's figure. She was clearly relishing the present tableau: the Serious Actress having dinner with the Serious Playwright — *dans une brasserie*, no less!, talking about a Serious Play. She was even attempting to strike some kind of preppy-bohemian-off-Broadway pose, wearing a man's oxford shirt and jeans, and with her hair pulled back. At the same time, some equal and opposite impulse had caused her to apply lipstick and eyeliner and to leave her shirt largely unbuttoned, revealing a glorious expanse of neck and upper chest. The result was the Bimbo Intellectual look; you know, the knockout who, in the second half of the movie, turns out to have a Ph.D. in Physics and, therefore, is the only one who can defuse the bomb.

After the food, which I barely touched, what with my nerves, Sarabeth reached into her bag and pulled out a copy of the play along with a pencil and pair of glasses. She put on the glasses and lodged the pencil into her hair.

"First off," she said, "I just want to say, I love the whole emphasis on the sense of smell. I think it's the most provocative of the senses."

She meant "evocative," of course, but I ignored the mistake. The glasses, I decided, were non-prescription, just clear glass meant to complete the Bimbo Intellectual look. "Speaking of smells," I said, "I don't mean to be rude or anything, but are you using some unusual brand of shampoo or perfume or something?"

"Yeah! Wow! You really are into smells, aren't you? I'm using this stuff my trainer recommended? It's shampoo and body lotion made with sea kelp. It's supposed to be really good for you. It's nothing fancy, really, it's basically seaweed."

The camera zoomed in on Sarabeth's face, while the sound effects man turned on the echo chamber: "seaweed, seaweed, seaweed." And then, a shock cut to Gabriel's reaction, his slack jaw slowly repeating, "seaweed?"

"That's right," Sarabeth said pertly, "seaweed. You know, maybe that's a good smell for the play? Maybe we could work it into the script?"

"Yes."

She began flipping through the play, stopping here and there to make comments. "Even though the smells are so important, Gabriel? I can definitely see places where my character should speak a few lines, don't you think?"

"Yes," I said, for I was scarcely aware of what I was saying. I kept getting whiffs of seaweed, the smell of my past and my future. It was the smell I had been searching for throughout my youth. As it happened, Sarabeth even resembled my mother, in the sense that they were both women. The point was, I had to get closer to that smell. I had to fill my lungs with it. This was not a matter of rational volition, any more than breathing is a matter of choice. It was a life-or-death issue of getting my nose next to her hair and skin.

Elated By Details

Sarabeth pointed to a page of script. "Here, for example. Don't you think this would be a perfect place for—" I quickly leaned across the table, hoping I could "inadvertently" stick my nose into her hair, but she just as quickly leaned back.

"You know what?" I said. "This is awkward, working on a script across the table like this. Why don't I move over to your side?"

Before she could answer, I was sitting beside her on the banquette, already getting a stronger dose of seaweed. "The thing is," Sarabeth was saying, "I think it's important that the audience understand that my character is a woman who's had to overcome a lot of obstacles—"

"Absolutely, absolutely," I said. God only knows what she was talking about. I turned toward Sarabeth, but pretended to be looking beyond her, scanning the back of the restaurant. "Hey look over there," I said. "I think that's Neil Simon." When she turned around to look, I would discreetly lean over and get a good nose-full of her scent.

"Who's Neil Simon?" she said, without turning around.

"He's a famous playwright," I said sharply. "You've got to be able to recognize people like him if you're going to be involved in theater. Go ahead, look over there."

She turned around. I began to slide over toward her. She quickly turned back to me and said, "Well, which one is he?"

I stopped my sliding. Of course, Neil Simon was not in the restaurant, so I could not point him out. But wait! She didn't even know who he was, so I could make up anything.

85

"Over there," I said, "way in the corner? He's the tall guy with the beard."

She strained to get a good look at him. I leaned toward her, put my nose as close as possible to the back of her head, and breathed in. This was the smell that had been shut tight in the vault of my memory. I exhaled away from her, and then breathed in again, my nose placed just above the barrette that was holding her hair back.

"It's funny," said Sarabeth as she began to turn herself back around, "but he looks like—"

I had not reacted quickly enough. By the time she turned around, our faces were millimeters apart. "Um. Hello?" she said.

"Sorry," I said, still breathing in deeply through my nose. "I was just trying to get a good look at him."

"Could you move over a little?"

I slid away from her. "I was just saying," Sarabeth continued, "that Neil Simon guy looks a lot like one of my dad's business partners."

"Everyone has a double."

I had chosen badly, for the bearded man had just paid his check and was now making to leave the restaurant. As he walked toward the door, his eye caught our table and he immediately detoured.

"Hey Carol!" the bearded man said to his wife. "Look: it's Sarabeth Lycasin! Sarabeth, how *are* you?"

"I'm doing great, Mr. Wallace. I thought I recognized you!"

Elated By Details

This was, indeed, one of her father's business partners. Sarabeth introduced me as an up-and-coming playwright. Wallace offered me his hand, which I accepted into my own sweating palm.

Sarabeth continued. "I'm going to be asking Dad to try to line up some backers for Gabriel's new play. I'm going to be the lead — if Gabriel will let me."

"The — there's no question—" I spluttered.

"That sounds promising," Wallace's wife said.

"You know what?" Sarabeth said to Wallace. "Gabriel says you're the spitting image of a famous playwright yourself—"

"You know," I said, "now that I see him up close—"

"Really?" said Wallace, addressing himself to Sarabeth. "Which playwright?"

"Some guy named Neil Simon?"

"Me? But I don't look anything like Neil Simon." He proceeded to describe Neil Simon.

"Must have been a trick of the eye," I said.

"Are you sure you're in the right profession?" said Wallace. "I mean, if you think I'm Neil Simon. Well, I just don't know." The Wallaces left, both of them regarding me suspiciously.

"What's the deal with that?" said Sarabeth. "Were you, like, trying to embarrass me or something?"

"It's a common mistake," I said. "Your Mr. Wallace must have been thinking of *Paul* Simon. He's the short, dumpy guy. *Neil* Simon is the tall, bearded one. People get them mixed up all the time."

"I don't know about that. Mr. Wallace is a pretty sharp guy."

"Let's go back to the play," I said, as earnestly as possible. "We should really get some of your ideas down on paper while they're still fresh. Frankly, I can't believe you're new to the theater of the avant-garde, Sarabeth. Your whole perspective is so cerebral — it's like Stoppard and Fugard, with a touch of Ionesco."

That seemed to work. "Well, I hope you know those guys better than Neil Simon," she said with a smile.

"Infinitely so," I said. "Why don't we get out of this restaurant? Don't you live nearby?"

"Yes, but—" That she was bashful, rather than indignant, told me I was making the right move. Soon enough, I would be alone with her and her seaweed scented body.

I adopted a masterful tone: "Yes, Sarabeth?"

"Nothing, Gabriel. It's just. Don't you like it here?"

"You know what? I'm not liking the karma in this restaurant. Sorry, it's the artist's temperament. You know what it's like."

"Okay, we'll go to my place."

She paid the check. I pantomimed as though I intended to pay, but she insisted, as I knew she would. Soon, we were inside her apartment, sitting next to each other on the sofa, poring over the play, which sat on the coffee table. With enough flattery — really, I should have been an actor, not a writer — I was able to make up for the embarrassment of

Elated By Details

the restaurant and begin building up some good will.

In no time, we were writing long soliloquies for Sarabeth's character. They would ruin the play, absolutely destroy it. No matter. To hell with art. This play would make Sarabeth a Serious Actress and, in her gratitude, she would fall in love me. I was making a large down payment on the erotic house I was building in my mind. Sarabeth and I would live a life of wanton lust, our days and nights spent rolling around in vats of warm seaweed lotion.

When I asked for a drink, Sarabeth apologized that she had no alcohol, and suggested we have cocaine instead. I agreed, eager to show I would be as much at home at your crazy Malibu parties as I was in your Upper West Side salons. It was my first time doing cocaine, and a couple "lines" of the stuff hit me like a quadruple espresso. I was still myself, of course, only more so.

"Hey!" I said, nodding my head in anticipatory agreement with what I was about to say. "We forgot all about the whole *seaweed* thing. We have to find a way to work that *seaweed* smell into the play. We can add it to the scratch-n-sniff card and everything."

"Cool."

"Do you have any of it here?" I said. "I need it for inspiration."

She ran to the bathroom and returned with the sea kelp body lotion. She waved the bottle under my nose. Good thing I was sitting down.

"I just love this stuff," she said, putting a little on her

hands and rubbing some on her arms and neck. Then she gave me the bottle. "Try some yourself."

I dabbed some lotion on my face; the fumes were enough to send me halfway to the womb. My world was now reduced to the small area of Sarabeth's exposed flesh, flanked by her partially open shirt. To open that shirt all the way would be as natural as pulling apart the curtains in my room. And then, to kiss her breasts, and then her stomach, and then lower and lower.

"What are you thinking about?" she said.

"This smell," I said. "This is fundamental. This is the smell of the sea. All life comes from the sea, ultimately. Did you know the composition of human blood is almost identical to that of seawater? And the Freudians say the sea is the most common metaphor for sex. It's because the sea is caressing and violent at the same time. And because a human being can melt into the sea, the sea and the person become one. The tides and the waves are like a constant, throbbing sensuality. Sarabeth, the sea is like a restless tongue that keeps lapping Mother Earth!"

"Whoa! That's pretty hot stuff," she said, laughing. "It's making me kinda hot!"

"I want you," I said. I lunged toward her and took her in my arms. "I want to melt into you, like the sea!" I began to cover her face and neck with big sloppy kisses. The scene was exactly perfect, but for one small detail: she screamed "rape" at the top of her lungs. And then again: "Help! Rape! Help! Rape!"

Elated By Details

Apparently, Sarabeth had had trouble with "stalkers" in the past and, therefore, employed a security guard who was, at that moment, watching CNN in the maid's room. In five seconds, he was in the living room. In seven seconds, he was kneeling on top of my chest. Once it was clear I was not going to offer any resistance, the security guard called the police.

Sarabeth retreated to her bedroom, emerging only when the cops arrived. She gave a brief statement to the effect that I was nuts, that I had tried to rape her, and, had it not been for the security guard, I would have succeeded. I was escorted to the local precinct, where I was booked and fingerprinted. The whole process was fascinating, except when I remembered that I was the subject of it. I was then driven across town to a "holding cell" while my paperwork was processed and the cops and prosecutors decided whether I was to be charged with attempted rape, or some lesser misdemeanor. The law-and-order bureaucracy being what it is, I spent the whole evening in the foul-smelling lock-up.

Early in the morning, I was told the charge would be misdemeanor assault rather than attempted rape. There was a brief arraignment before a judge at which it was established that I had no record, lived with my grandmother, and had, at the very least, been invited into Sarabeth's apartment even if I allegedly took some liberties while there. I was released on my own recognizance pending trial.

Afterwards, I stood outside the courthouse and stared at the traffic passing by. It seemed to me that each car, even the ones with that nice new-car smell, were driving themselves to oblivion. Like lemmings to the sea, they followed the creature in front of them, unaware they were skirting the edge of a precipice. Who was driving? It made no difference—a bunch of self-deluded fools. Let them tumble into the sea and crash upon the rocks. My thoughts were filled with cruelty.

And then I remembered that it was Saturday, and that made me happy. I was taking Roseanne to the Rainbow Room that evening. She would smell of Obsession.

THE SECRET PASSION OF AN ARTIST

Jean Paul made one final, bold brushstroke and stood back from the canvas. He shrugged his shoulders, put down the palette, and said to the model, "That will be all for today, Lucretia."

Lucretia wrapped a silk kimono around her perfect young body and delicately cleared her throat. "Ah-hem."

"Yes?" said Jean Paul.

"I don't mean to be nosy," said Lucretia, "but we've worked together for a few years and, lately, I get the feeling your heart isn't really in this."

Jean Paul checked to make sure they were alone and then sat down wearily on an old crate. "I wonder, Lucretia, whether my heart ever was in painting."

"But then, why did you go into it?"

"The usual reasons," he said, lighting a cigarette. "My father did it. It seemed like an honorable profession, etcetera, etcetera."

Lucretia helped herself to a glass of the Beaujolais that Jean Paul always had on offer. "It was the same with me and modeling. My mother was an artist's model and it just seemed like the path of least *résistance*," she said, finishing the sentence with gallic flair.

"Just between you and me, Lucretia, I plan to get out of this business."

"Ah hah! Are you one of those men with a secret life? An artist by day, but—"

"That's right," said Jean Paul. "I only paint so I can pay the bills. But what I really am is an aspiring lawyer!"

"That's incredible!" said Lucretia. "But law? Are you sure you can put up with the risks, the uncertainties? There are safer ways to get out of painting."

"Safety!" cried Jean Paul, stubbing out his cigarette. "I've been playing it safe all my life—going to art school, taking an entry-level position in the impressionism department, working my way up through cubism and abstract expressionism. It's all so damn predictable!"

"I know what you mean," said Lucretia. "This business of being an artist's model is so tedious! The flowers, the perfume, the jewelry from worshipful men, the constant love affairs with, quote, fascinating young artists, the hours and hours of sitting in cafes. And what does it get you in the end? A managing director position in the modeling depart-

Elated By Details

ment and a big fat pension. There must be more to life."

"Exactly! One has to get off the treadmill. I've thought about other career tracks. I could always get a position in a poetry factory or a novel writing company. Sure, the money would be good, but it wouldn't satisfy my soul any more than painting. What can I say? When people look at me, they see an artist, but deep down, I'm a lawyer."

"How do you find the time to pursue law, what with a full-time artist's schedule?"

"In the evenings," said Jean Paul. "I've been going to law school classes. You should see the other students! They're just like me, stuck in dead-end artistic jobs, yearning to know this thing called 'law.'"

"I'll let you in on a secret," said Lucretia, twirling a strand of blond hair around a finger. "I've been training to be a waitress."

Jean Paul stood up. "Lucretia, that's wonderful! I apologize — I've always thought of you as just another stunningly beautiful nude model. I had no idea that you were a closet waitress."

"Well, I'm still not sure I should take the plunge."

"But Lucretia, if you really have food service skills, what a tragedy to let them go to waste. Think of all the great waitresses this country has produced, you could be one of them!"

"Yes, but I have to be realistic. I'm not independently wealthy. I can't just run off and become a waitress. How would I pay the rent?"

The room fell silent, but for the faint sound of the Edith Piaf's voice in the background. Jean Paul lit another cigarette and poured himself a glass of wine. At last he turned to her. "What if you only had to pay half the rent?"

"You mean—?"

"That's right. *Cohabitation*. We could start a new life together. Just imagine — you, devoting yourself full-time to waiting tables; me, practicing law."

"You mad fool! What would we live on?"

"We'd scrape by. Hell, if things got tough, I could always do some part-time painting."

"I know we've had numerous love affairs, Jean Paul, but I always assumed you were a typical artist; just blowing off steam as you climbed the ladder of success. I never thought it actually meant anything to you."

"I'm afraid I have feelings for you, Lucretia. I guess I'm one of those 'sensitive lawyer' types. Late at night I find myself composing briefs and affidavits about you. Go ahead and laugh if you want to."

"I'm not going to laugh, Jean Paul. Now that I know you're an aspiring lawyer, I can finally tell you how I feel about you."

"Could it be—?"

"Yes. I've never told you before, but I keep having this dream—" Lucretia's eyes misted over. "In the dream, I've finally made it as a waitress and you're my customer. I'm reading you the daily specials, and the list just keeps going on and on, because I don't want to stop!"

Elated By Details

"Here, dry your eyes," said Jean Paul, handing her a box of tissues. "Let's stop dreaming, Lucretia. Let's live together."

"Where would we live? These draughty fifth-floor walk-up garrets are so expensive, but this is where everybody lives!"

"We're not like other people, you and me. We'll move to the suburbs. Out there, you can get a split level and a quarter acre for a song. I'll get rid of this damn beret and pretend I never lived this hollow existence."

"This is all so sudden," said Lucretia. "I think I'm getting cold feet. Are you sure you wouldn't rather continue having affairs with me and various other nude models?"

"No," said Jean Paul. "I know that's what society dictates, but I don't care anymore. I'm sorry, Lucretia, but I want monogamy. Maybe even marriage!"

Lucretia gasped. "Won't your family be furious?"

"The true lawyer has no family," said Jean Paul. "I will live for my work, drafting wills and trust indentures, even if it doesn't make me a dime! I ask you: do you want to be part of that life?"

"Yes! Yes! A thousand times, yes!" cried Lucretia, her eyes burning with love. "Let's have sex, right now!"

"Not until we're married."

And as they embraced, Lucretia knew life with Jean Paul would never be boring.

A REGULAR DON JUAN

I don't know about you, but whenever somebody asks me to "set an example," it usually backfires. Something inside me just makes me want to smoke, or drink, or do whatever it is I'm not supposed to be doing.

If you ask me to set an example of good sportsmanship, I'll probably cheat. If you ask me to set an example of good manners, I'll be rude. Michelle did something even worse: she asked me to set an example of a good boyfriend.

And Michelle wasn't even my girlfriend. She was my ex-girlfriend, now happily married to some nonentity who just happened to be the youngest managing director in investment banking history. In the perverse way women occasionally have, Michelle got along famously with my current girlfriend, Eve. Michelle and Eve had recruited me

Elated By Details

to help one of their mutual friends, Isabel, who found herself in an unhappy marriage with a guy named Miles Glideright.

Miles and Isabel had been living in Boston, where Miles was doing his surgical residency. Miles had apparently been something of a Don Juan, and after repeated infidelities, Isabel had asked for a separation. But now, Miles had obtained a fellowship at a big New York hospital, and he and Isabel had decided to move to Manhattan and give their marriage one more chance. That's when Eve and Michelle hatched the idea of throwing a "couples weekend" at Michelle's house in East Hampton. The idea was: if we "happy" couples could set an example for Miles and Isabel, it might help them to patch things up.

Eve and I took the Jitney from Manhattan to East Hampton. She read a magazine and I stared out the window, wondering how I could escape from this unsolicited role of an exemplary boyfriend. By the last stage of the journey, the taxi ride to Michelle's, I was already beginning to rebel.

"Hey Eve," I said when the taxi came to a stop, "would you mind paying the guy?"

"You know, honey," she said, "I love the way you treat me like an equal. Not always paying for everything or opening doors all the time."

"Would you mind carrying my bag?" I said.

"And I love your sense of humor!"

That was Eve in a nutshell. There was no way to get through to her. No way to convey the supreme ambivalence in my soul, an ambivalence being compounded by Michelle's insistence on labeling us as a "happy" couple. Of course, I knew it was high time for me to get married, and I knew Eve was the perfect woman for me, and I also knew she would say "yes" if I only asked her — and, frankly, all that pressure was making me sullen and bad tempered. These impulses were well under way that first night at East Hampton, when I sat brooding in the corner of one of the guest bedrooms.

"What are you doing?" said Eve. She had just emerged from the bathroom having brushed her teeth and washed her face. She was wearing some kind of slinky black nightshirt she had acquired specially to add a dash of romance to the weekend.

"Smoking and drinking," I said.

"That's not like you," she said.

"I know. I'm just thinking about this Miles guy. He's quite a character."

"Creep is the word I would use," said Eve. "But I can see why Isabel fell for him. He is a good-looking man."

I folded my arms across my chest in the manner of one grievously hurt, "I'm so glad he turns you on."

"I didn't say that," said Eve. "He's not as good looking as you, honey."

I grunted. Even I could see Miles was better looking than me, but that hardly seemed like the right pretext for the argument I was trying to pick. I tried a different tack: "Michelle told me Isabel once caught Miles having a threesome with a couple of nurses from the hospital."

"Really?"

"Uh huh." The room fell silent for a moment. Then I said, "Hey, I don't suppose you would ever consider doing something like, you know—"

"Henry!" Eve blushed. And then she walked across the room and sat down beside me. "Well, I guess if it were really important to you, and if you found a woman who was really attractive, I guess I'd be willing to try anything once."

"Oh, that's great!" I cried. "So, I'm not exciting enough. Now you want to have sex with other people!" I was in a mood, alright.

"I didn't say I wanted to do it," said Eve, "although I'll admit I'm as curious as the next person. But really, I would only do it if it were important to you. I just don't want us to end up like Miles and Isabel. I don't want you to feel like you have to go elsewhere if you want to indulge some harmless fantasy about threesomes."

"I didn't say I had a thing about threesomes," I said bitterly.

"We are going to stay together, aren't we Henry?"

I grunted again.

Eve ran her hand up my thigh. "Come on, honey, let's see how much fun we can have as a twosome."

I stood up. "What do you want from me? You want me to make all kinds of promises to you! And all you want to do is have sex and fantasize about threesomes? What kind of man wants a woman like that?"

The evening ended in tears, and with Eve issuing me my walking papers. I slept on the living room sofa and, the next morning, caught the Jitney back to Manhattan.

* * *

For a few days, I was surprisingly bucked up. I felt the rush of blessed freedom. No more ball and chain! No more craven promises extracted at moments of weakness! No more annoying inquiries from relatives: when are you crazy kids going to tie the knot, eh?

But then the first weekend came, and I began to have second thoughts about the whole break-up. I looked for friends with whom to carouse, but being 35 and single, I was running short on people to play with. My erstwhile friends were always doing things like getting married, having babies, changing diapers — all part of their campaign to pressure me into matrimony.

I began a slow descent into melancholy. On Saturday afternoon, I was settling down to a six-pack of Sam Adams, a carton of Lucky Strikes, and what promised to be a deliciously miserable evening. With any luck, I would get drunk enough and lonely enough to call Eve and make a complete fool of myself.

My apartment is on the ground floor of an old walk-up with two sash windows facing East 92nd Street. I was having my beer and cigarettes on a chair next to one of the win-

Elated By Details

dows when the phone rang. I picked up immediately.

"Eve?"

"Listen, old boy. I need your help."

I knew immediately the voice belonged to Miles, with whom I had exchanged numbers in East Hampton. Still, I was ticked off that he didn't bother to identify himself. I was also ticked off that he didn't have the decency to be Eve instead of Miles.

"And you are—?" I said, sounding a little like the doorman of a fancy club.

"Oh, right, it's Miles. Sorry, I always forget to say that part. People sometimes hang up when they hear the name. But that's not important. The reason I called was to see if you could give me a hand moving?" This was evidently Miles' way of being ingratiating — turning everything into a question. "Um, Isabel kind of threw me out?" Miles then convulsed with a manic laughter.

"I'm sorry to hear that."

"Not to worry, old boy," he said, his laughter stopping as abruptly as it had started. "The thing is, I've got a shift at the hospital tonight, so I've got to get this move done today. I know it's last minute, but did you have other plans this afternoon?"

I hesitated.

"I would really love to help you, Miles, but I do have plans. I'm going to this dinner party. It's a pretty formal thing, so I can't back out. In fact, I've got to head over for cocktails pretty soon. I'm literally just tying my tie right now."

Miles laughed again. "That's not the way it looks to me."

That voice did not, as you might be thinking, come from the other end of the phone, but from just outside the window. There, on the sidewalk in front of my apartment was Miles. He was of medium height and powerfully built, carrying a cardboard box in one hand and a cell phone in the other. The sight of him startled me and made me spill beer all over my lap. I put the bottle down amidst a hail of expletives.

"Didn't mean to alarm you, old boy. Are you going to a dinner party dressed like that?"

"It's just that—"

"Never explain, old boy. Come on, I've got the car right out front."

"All right," I said, getting up from the chair.

* * *

It only took a few hours to move Miles into his new place: a small, but hip, studio in the East Village. As there was still time to kill before Miles began his shift at the hospital, he invited me for a drink.

"You drink before going to the hospital?"

"I have to, old boy, they don't let me drink *at* the hospital."

We wandered over to Alphabet City, and into one of the trendy bars that had opened up in recent years. Over crisp martinis, Miles told me the story of his final blow-up with Isabel. She had discovered him in bed with a medical student

Elated By Details

and sent him packing. Miles was one of those people who came to life with a drink or two. His gray eyes, which had been at half-mast before, now began darting this way and that.

"But enough about me," said Miles. "I gather the weekend in East Hampton was not a total success for you and Eve, either."

"No."

"Too bad. She's a hot one, old boy."

"Yes," I said pathetically.

"Oh well. So we're both bachelors," said Miles, his eyes beginning to roam the bar.

"I don't know," I said. "I think I made a mistake. I think I'm going to call Eve — maybe even tonight."

Miles nodded and took a sip of his drink. "Big mistake," he said.

"Why?"

"You don't want to go crawling back to a woman like that. She might take you back, but it'll never be the same. She won't respect you. I'll tell you what you should be doing. You should be parallel processing."

"Parallel what?"

"Parallel processing, multi-tasking — seeing other women."

"But I like Eve. I may even love her."

"All the more reason for you to see other women. Listen," he said, sitting down on a bar stool. "Women have intuition; they have sixth sense; they have 'gaydar,' they're basically witches, okay? One thing they pick up on right away is neediness — and it's a big turn-off. There's an invisible aura around a guy who already has a woman. Ever notice that once you start going out with one chick, you start getting second looks from all the others? And, you ever notice the way that women fawn all over married men? And married men with kids? Forget about it!" Miles said the last bit with a mock-Bowery accent. "Men in that position project confidence. So, if you want to get Eve back, then you have to get yourself another woman."

"Okay, I'll think about it."

"No time like the present, old boy. Pretty good talent around here," he said.

A woman walked past us, wearing a low-cut bodice-style shirt, showing ample cleavage. "Take her, for example," said Miles. "You know what the thing is about her? The shoes. Look at those shoes. Very strappy, very sexy."

"Just what I was thinking."

"Liar," he said. "You should pay attention to details. Women put a lot of effort into the details, Nothing turns them on more than if you notice. Here, follow me."

Miles walked over to the bodice woman, who was having drinks with a female friend, and said, "My friend and I have a little bet. He says your shoes are Blahnik, but I say they're Kélian."

The woman laughed. "Well, you're both wrong, they're knock-offs. What are you guys, designers?"

"No."

Elated By Details

"But you were standing there noticing my *shoes*? Now that's what I call refreshing!"

The woman's name was Alix, and she was a painter. Within a few minutes, Miles had her phone number and was promising to call her the following week. With a flourish, Miles finished his martini and announced. "Believe it or not, I have to go to work now! But it was great meeting you; I'll give you a call."

"My God, you work fast," I said as we left the bar. "So, are you going to call her?"

"Naw," he said. "You take it." He handed me the slip of paper with her phone number. "That was just an exercise for your benefit. By the way, you were supposed to be chatting up the other woman."

* * *

Alix greeted me with the words I feared the most: "You're the other guy."

I had phoned her and told her how much I had enjoyed meeting her. Nothing dishonest about that. I invited her to dinner and she accepted. We met at an artsy bistro on St. Mark's Place.

"Yes, I am the other guy," I said.

"What is this?" Alix said. "Some kind of bait-and-switch game you guys are playing?"

I was not an accomplished seducer like Miles, who had strategies to deal with every contingency. I had only one weapon in my arsenal. It was this: I spent part of my childhood in England and I have retained a certain residual Britishness that I can trot out when the need arises. Reliable friends have told me that, under the right conditions, my mannerisms bring to mind those of Hugh Grant in *Four Weddings and a Funeral*.

"Well, um," I said, taking off my glasses, "I, er, don't blame you for being deuced angry. But it wasn't a game, no, no, not-at-all, just a bit of crossed signals. You see, when Miles asked for your number, he was really doing it for me. As in myself. Actually, although you've come to think of me as the 'other guy,' it's really Miles who is the 'other guy.' In reality, I'm just the 'guy.'"

Alix smiled in a way that was not discouraging. I plowed on: "The thing is that I, er, oh dear, how shall I say this? I had been admiring you — well, worshipping, really — the whole evening, but I'm afraid I suffer from a, um, that is to say that I am, I am," I averted my eyes, "painfully shy."

"Really?" said Alix. "That's so sweet."

"Oh, thank you," I said. "But I can see it was beastly of me to ask you here. Shall I hail you a taxi?"

"No! I mean, we're here; let's have dinner. What did you say your name was?"

"Henry."

"It's funny, at first, I didn't even notice you were British. You seem like a really sweet guy, Henry."

Not bad, huh? The dinner was enjoyable, despite my having to remind myself to keep up the British accent.

Elated By Details

After dinner, I walked Alix to the loft building where she had a combination apartment-and-painting studio. Alix suggested I should come up "some time" and take a look at her paintings. But I didn't press my luck. I gave her a kiss on the cheek and told her I hoped we would get together soon.

All of this I was able to report to Miles the next time we met for drinks.

Miles asked me what I proposed to do.

"Call Alix and ask her on another date?" I ventured.

"That would be a serious mistake, old boy. The first lesson is: never call. I repeat: never call. Once you've got them interested in you? Stop calling. It drives them wild."

"Come on! She'll just think I'm a jerk."

"Wrong again. She'll blame herself! What is a woman," he mused, looking at the ceiling, "but a great bouncy bundle of insecurities? When you don't call her, she'll start to think, am I boring? And then she'll think, am I fat? Within a week, she'll be thinking, am I boring and fat? At some point, the uncertainty will be too much and she'll call you. That's when you can reassure her. Of course you're interested in her, it's just that you've been insanely-crazy-busy lately and haven't had time to pick up the phone. She'll be eating out of your hand."

"What if she doesn't call?"

"Then it wasn't gonna happen anyway."

A few days later, Alix left me a voicemail, which I did not answer. The next night, she reached me at home. "Didn't you get my earlier message?"

"Oh, er, yes," I said, removing my glasses, even though she couldn't see me over the phone. "It's just that I've been *insanely* busy these last few days."

"That's okay," she said, sweetly. "I just wanted to say that I'm sorry about the way I snapped the other night — that thing about the bait-and-switch. It was unfair of me. I really enjoyed our dinner and, I don't know, I thought maybe we could do something sometime, when you're not so busy?"

"But of course, pussycat!" I wanted to say, but I thought that might be laying it on too thick. Instead, I did a phone blush and said, "Oh golly! That would be lovely, I mean, if you really would like to see me again."

After our next dinner, Alix took me back to her place to see her paintings. They were large, blotchy, non-representational things. "It's very powerful," I said of one of her canvases. "It seems to represent the tragedy of Man."

"You mean, Man and Woman, don't you?"

I turned to her. "Man embraces Woman," I said, and we began to kiss, long, deep passionate kisses. I unbuttoned the top button of her shirt.

"No," she said. "Not tonight, Henry. It's too soon. I want the moment to be just right."

* * *

"That was a major strategic setback," said Miles, twirling a martini. "You let her turn the tables on you — now she's withholding something you want. Bad show, old

Elated By Details

boy. You're going to have to give her some major silent treatment now."

"What am I supposed to do in the meantime?" I asked.

"You're going to do what you should have been doing all along — parallel processing."

"Speaking of that," I said, "you wouldn't believe it, but I had a voicemail from Eve last night."

"Really? What did she say?"

"She said she missed me, and things like that. So, you know, I thought maybe I should call her back and see if she wants to get together."

"Have you learned nothing from me?" Miles said, and then broke into another one of his laughing fits. "Eve doesn't count as parallel processing! If you call her back right away, then it's obvious you don't have any other options. Whatever you do, don't call her. At this point, your attitude should be: 'hey, I'm a busy guy with lots of chicks, I don't have time to return every phone call from ex-girlfriends.'"

"Oh, right," I said. This business of being a cad was exhausting.

"Now," said Miles, "take a look down this bar. What are the most promising prospects?"

There seemed to be very few prospects. There were several couples at the bar; two older women earnestly conversing over glasses of white wine, an enormously fat woman buying drinks for what looked to be a group of co-workers, and two young blonds.

"The blonds?" I said.

"You're not very good at this, are you? No, it's the heavy chick. Look at her; she's attached to this whole crowd of young things. Think of her as the queen bee. Get in good with her, and she'll lead you into the beehive."

When we were standing next to the big woman, Miles said, "Excuse me, but I just wanted to say that it's totally amazing how you remembered all those drink orders. There must have been two-dozen different drinks, and you even remembered the liquor brands — Tanqueray and this, Stoli. Amazing! You used to be a waitress, right?"

She blushed. "Yeah, I used to waitress during the summer."

She was named Katie and she worked for a publishing house. Since we seemed like decent guys, Katie invited us to have a drink with her colleagues, one of whom was named Donna.

* * *

One week, and two voicemails from Alix, later, I was sitting at the bar of the Tribeca Grand, nursing a Sam Adams, when Donna finally showed up. She was wearing tight leather pants and very dark eyeliner. She gave me a rather intrigued look.

"You're the other guy," she said, and laughed.

"Of course I am, pussycat," I said. "I positively begged Miles for your number."

"Lose the accent," she said, "it's kind of creepy. You

should have told me you were the other guy."

"I know, but I was afraid you wouldn't come. The fact is, from the moment Katie introduced us, I haven't been able to stop thinking about you. If you feel you've been cheated, you're free to go."

Donna shrugged. "No biggie. It's not like I know either of you. Besides, you're kind of cute." She suddenly got a wild look in her eye.

We went to see a film with subtitles and then went for more drinks at a Latino bar. After a couple of Pisco Sours, Donna got that wild look back in her eyes. In a dark corner of the bar, we started kissing.

"So," she said. "Are you straight or bi?"

"Straight, as far as I know."

"It's a trick question," she said. "I believe everybody is bisexual, whether they realize it or not."

"You mean you're—?"

"You better believe it," she said. "Not that I'm really practicing, if you know what I mean. But I'm sure I've got it in me."

And there I saw the answer to all my problems. I saw the means to sweep away all of my frustrations, to join the league of men like Miles, and even a way to get back to Eve who, in the final analysis, was the woman I should have been with the whole time.

After all, Eve said she was "as curious as the next person." And she would be willing to indulge me in "harmless" fantasies. It was only a few weeks since we split up. Surely this would be the perfect occasion to bring her back into my life and put our relationship on a much more exciting footing.

I leered at Donna. "It might be interesting to experiment," I said. "Have you ever thought about a threesome?"

"Sure," she said. "But it's hard to find the right people. There has to be attraction all around."

Jackpot! "Well, we seem to be attracted to each other, for starters. And I know a very hot woman who'll join us."

That silenced her for a moment. I had called her bluff. I was afraid she would back out. Instead, she got that wild look again.

"Okay," she said. "But fair's fair. There's no law that says a threesome has to be two women. First, we're going to do it with two boys. After that, I'll do it with you and your girl."

"Ouch," I said, for she had grabbed my crotch.

"Do you know any nice boys?"

"Not off-hand," I gasped. She let go.

"Well, you'd better find one."

*　*　*

Finding a suitable man for a *ménage à trois* is easier said than done. Although I considered myself to be straight, it seemed to me the second man ought to be either bisexual or gay to make the thing work. Ideally, I wanted a man who would be sufficiently interested in me to give Donna a little thrill, which would then make her want to insert herself

Elated By Details

between the two of us.

My search for the right man consumed my free time. I let Alix slide off into oblivion. I spent fruitless hours researching the *Village Voice* personals. And then, just as I was about to abandon hope, the answer appeared to me, plain as the nose on my face, so to speak.

At my law firm, there was a junior associate named Barry who had always struck me as having a rather ambiguous sexuality. Barry was thin, with a sensuous mouth and straw colored hair that flopped over one eye. Had he been female, he'd have been a beautiful woman. He was also in the habit of stopping by my office to ask trifling questions of professional conduct, which I had long suspected to be a form of flirtation.

I took Barry out for a beer after work. He was delighted to be bonding with me for I was a senior associate, widely rumored to be on the fast track to partnership. I took a long sip of beer, set down the frosty mug, and turned to Barry. "It's good to have a night with the boys, don't you agree?"

Barry nodded.

"You wanna know something?" I said. "I've been seeing this chick—" I shot a glance at Barry. Was that disappointment on his face?

"She's a real piece of work," I continued, laughing heartily. "She wants us to experiment, you know, sexually. She wants us to tap into our own latent bisexuality, as she puts it. Can you believe it?"

Barry smiled nervously.

"Just the other day, she said 'let's do a threesome.' Just like that! At first, I'm thinking, no. That's too weird for me. But, you know, lately I've been thinking, with the right partners, it could be a really eye-opening experience. What do you think?"

Barry looked into his beer. "Sure, I guess."

"So you think I should go for it?"

"If that's what you want to do. I guess so."

"I've been trying to find out more about this whole threesome racket. I was wondering: have you ever done anything like that, Barry?"

"No."

"But you are kind of curious, aren't you?"

He looked over his shoulder and whispered. "I don't know. That's kind of an awkward question, Henry." He was being so coy, like a shy woodland creature. It was almost alluring.

"Look Barry, let me make this easy. I want you to join me and Donna. Just because you and I work together, doesn't mean we can't be friends outside of the office. I've seen the way you look at me, the way you stop by my office on any flimsy pretext. Well, I must admit, it's very flattering even though that kind of thing isn't my usual scene. I guess I'm saying, why not explore our real feelings toward each other? I don't think this will hurt our working relationship. Quite the contrary, really."

The next day, Barry reported me for sexual harassment and I was summarily fired. I tried to get another job, but with

Elated By Details

my old firm refusing to give me a favorable recommendation, I received no offers. I went on unemployment insurance and started eating macaroni and cheese. In the meantime, Donna took matters into her own hands, and recruited a gay friend of hers who was willing to try a threesome.

The three of us met at the apartment of Donna's friend, whose name was John. John did his best to get everyone in the mood with soft lights, thumping music, and lots of booze. It was a disaster. John had no interest in Donna and I had no interest in John. I *was* interested in Donna. The sight of her naked was not disappointing, but it was impossible to perform while another man was in the room. Feeling I'd let everyone down, I offered myself to John. He made various attempts on me, using lubricants and paraphernalia that, under other circumstances, might have made me laugh. It was not long until he realized how unwilling I was. He gave up, saying I was making him feel like a rapist.

The evening, though brief, contained enough ambiguity, hurt, self-loathing, and shame to give me "issues" I continue to discuss with a very nice therapist named Stephen. In the depression that followed immediately upon that evening, I stopped shaving and started drinking rather heavily so as to forget the trauma of the threesome, as well as my recent firing.

For a few days I lost touch with Donna. Finally, I found her number under a pile of dirty laundry and called her.

She seemed glad to hear from me. "I was wondering how you were," she said.

"I'm fine," I said, washing down the last of my Percocets with a warm beer. "By the way, when are we going to have the second half of our little adventure?"

"Are you serious? The first half was kind of a horror show, wasn't it?"

"It wasn't so bad," I said. "Besides, fair's fair. You promised."

"Okay," she said. "If your friend is still into it, I'm willing. Let's do it."

I thought for a minute about whether to call Eve or just show up at her apartment. Notwithstanding the beer and painkillers, I could think clearly enough to see, given the circumstances of our break-up, I would have to speak to her in-person to set things right. In fact, I was possessed of this sense of momentum that told me I had to see her right away. I considered having a shower or a shave, but it was already getting late.

I left my apartment and started walking to Eve's place, which was on the West Side. When I got to Central park, a light summer rain started to fall. I didn't mind it, really. It was a kind of happy, playful rain, like the spritz of champagne that greets a winning athlete. The rain didn't do much to sober me up, unfortunately. I fell down a couple of times in the park, and by the time I got to Eve's apartment, I was soaked, with bits of mud and grass sticking to me.

Eve opened the door and let out a little gasp.

"Henry?"

I guess I didn't look quite myself. She, on the other hand,

Elated By Details

looked even better than I had remembered. She was wearing a black strapless cocktail dress and her fiery red hair hung provocatively about her bare shoulders. Her favorite eau de cologne wafted across the threshold. At that moment, I swear, I forgot all about the threesome. A completely different speech came into my head. "Eve," I was going to say, "forgive me for being such an ass. I was a fool to break up with you and I'm here to beg forgiveness. The fact is, I've always loved you, but the Peter Pan inside me couldn't make a commitment; he was too afraid of growing up. Well, I'm over all that now. I want to be with you—forever."

But before I could say any of that, a voice came from within the apartment. "Hey, babe? Where do you keep the corkscrew?" The voice sounded a lot like Miles.

PLODGETT REVISITED

Claudia had summed it up nicely. "What," she asked, "would make you drop everything and race across town?"

What she meant was: what are my passions? When nothing came out of my mouth, she put down her Campari and orange, smiled, and waved her hand in a gesture of explication. "I mean, you know, a concert, or an exhibition, or a film by a certain director?"

I sat there looking stupid, thinking, "I'm a lawyer; I work all the time. I can't just drop everything and race across town!" That train of thought momentarily fueled my aversion to rich, leisured types like Claudia, who take such infuriating pride at the fact that they can clear off their "busy" schedules — Busy? With what? What? — to attend every performance of the Ring cycle at the Met. Hey, and

Elated By Details

excuse me, but some of us work for a living.

It had been a brilliant spring day, much like today, with the sun glancing off the shiny cars of the Upper East Side. I remember the hush of the restaurant, the white tablecloth, the heavy silverware, and the obsequious waiter — all contributing to the clandestine nature of the thing. Claudia wore a turquoise dress, handmade from the best Thai silk, a pearl necklace that looked to be a family heirloom, and rather discreet earrings. She had a lazy voluptuousness that owed everything to breeding, nothing to exercise.

She repeated: "What would make you drop everything and race across town?"

"Maybe I'm not the impulsive type," I said.

"Wrong answer!" she said, and then giggled.

Yes, that was definitely the wrong answer. It is only now, two years later, that I may be able to give her the right answer. Perhaps it's not too late. Claudia is expecting me at one, and it's almost that now. But I know better than to show up at Claudia's flat on time. And so I wander over to Madison Avenue and sit in a coffee shop, turning memories over in my mind.

* * *

Claudia came into my life as a dinner companion at Malcolm's wedding. Malcolm was a successful journalist and he seemed to know positively everybody in Manhattan, as positively everybody liked to say. It was during the fish course that Claudia turned to me and said, in a voice that was equal parts New and Old England: "And what did you think of the ceremony?"

"I found it *so* derivative."

She laughed, and her big eyes gave off just a hint of derangement: "Oh, I agree — no prizes for originality here! Just the same old 'sickness and heath, better or worse' sort of thing!"

"More wine?"

"Yes, I suppose," she said. "Although what one really wants is champagne."

"One does, doesn't one?" I said. "By the way, I'm Phillip Twersky." I looked at her place card. "And you must be Claudia Plodgett."

"That's right."

"Not of the Boston Plodgetts?" I said, in mock drawing room voice.

"The same," she said.

"Seriously? As in Senator Plodgett, and Ambassador Plodgett-Smythe?"

"Yes."

"And Plodgett's Canned Soup?"

"A distant relation."

"And—" I stopped myself, cleared my throat, and tugged at my black tie. "And what have you got to say for yourself, anyway?"

"One wants champagne rather badly."

"I'm afraid that's how you'll get it," I said, and flagged

Elated By Details

down a waiter. The waiter explained, however, that champagne would only be served during the dessert course, when toasts were to be made. I excused myself and sprinted off to the bar of the Club where the wedding was being held. At first, the bartender refused to sell me a bottle of champagne on the ground, this being a private club, money should not change hands. On further negotiation, it turned out he meant only very large sums of money should change hands.

These were extraordinary lengths for a bottle of sparkling wine, but it gave me a secret thrill to be running an errand for a Plodgett. The Plodgetts, of course, were one of Boston's oldest families, equally at home in the pages of American history texts and the gossip columns of your better magazines. They were forever getting elected to Congress, nominated for the Supreme Court, or married off to European aristocrats. Anyway, to cut a long story short, the bartender and I settled on a price and I returned triumphant with the champers.

A week later, we met for our first lunch — the one where Claudia asked me about my passions.

* * *

"One did rather enjoy that," she said, rolling over on the bed and kissing my cheek.

"So did one," I said.

It was now three weeks since that first lunch, and most of the intervening time had been spent getting to this point.

There had been quite a series of lunches, cocktails, and dinners before we found ourselves in the state of clothelessness for which I had longed. Included in the price was learning all about Claudia's passions. Those things for which she would drop everything and rush across town. The list was daunting: Japanese gardens, Spanish majolica, Scottish castles, Austrian pastries, and Italian shoes, for starters.

"French kisses?" I suggested, but to no avail.

For my part, I remained depressingly bereft of passions. Perhaps it was Claudia's incessant talk of passions that made me feel so passionless. There is a certain dread of being put "on the spot" people like me have. When asked to name my favorite book I can never remember a single book I've read.

Claudia described in rapturous terms a motorcycle trip she once took from Rome to Ostia. The scenery was glorious. "Although," she added, "the motorcycling part did leave one rather sore."

"That happens all the time," I said. "It's called Ostiaporosis." Comments like that were mere defensive mechanisms for I still could not answer that question: "what would make you drop everything and race across town?" Nor did I have the wits to say, as some people might, "I've never been to Ostia myself, but Poughkeepsie, now there's a town," or something like that. Instead, I would make a mental note to come up with a list of passions for our next meeting.

Finally, after I'd made it through the preliminary rounds

Elated By Details

with Claudia, I planned the *denouement*: an expensive dinner at a French restaurant near my apartment. We had too much to drink and I led her back to my place. But Claudia had taken one look at the 1970's apartment building and refused to enter. She took my hand, hailed a cab, and whisked me up to her place just off Park Avenue. It was a tiny jewel-box of an apartment; basically a walk-in closet with a bed attached.

"It's really just one's *pied-à-terre*," Claudia said.

"Then shouldn't we be *en déshabillé*?"

She took the hint, and before we could empty our brandy snifters we were frantically undressing each other. "This is madness!" she whispered, which I took to be a line from an old movie. I answered in kind.

"I'm scared, but it's wonderful!"

She surrendered herself and when I was on top of her, I couldn't help thinking — I must confess — something along the lines of: I'm screwing a Plodgett! The whole enterprise was really bringing out the class warrior in me. I had subdued the owners of the means of production. And now that I held this power, what was I going to do? Join them, of course.

And so I drifted off to sleep, dreaming of the life to which I could now aspire: me, Phillip Plodgett — in my dream, men took their wives' name — the Lord of Plodgett Manor. After a hard day of fox hunting I would come home to a lavish dinner, followed by port and Stilton and then, still wearing our hunting pinks, of course, a wife-swapping party with the crowned heads of Europe. As the *paparazzi* clicked away, I would delight hereditary German princes with my quips: "You spend hours waiting for a Thurn-und-Taxi, and then two of them show up at once!"

The next morning, Claudia announced she was leaving for Europe that very evening. The words had little impact on me. Our union was a fact no mere transitory holiday could change. Even when she told me she would be gone all summer, I took it in stride. I made her a pot of strong tea while she packed her bags. As I poured her a cupper — one lump, dash of milk — I once again felt the thrill of being able to serve a Plodgett.

"Phillip," she said, her eyes darting back and forth, "while I'm gone—"

Write to me every day? Make preparations for our wedding? Convert to Christianity?

"...you won't mention this to anyone, will you?"

"No. Of course not."

She smiled. "I will miss those eyes of yours. You do have rather amazing eyes."

"Does one?"

* * *

Malcolm told me to get a grip. "Forget about Claudia," he said, as we ate dinner at an Italian restaurant in the Village. Something about his tone made me think he'd been down this road before. "She's going to marry somebody

Elated By Details

rich, and with an impeccable pedigree. And when she does get married, it isn't going to have anything to do with sex. That's why she's being so promiscuous now."

She is not! I inwardly screamed, and challenged Malcolm to a duel for good measure. But his words gradually sunk in. Over the next few weeks, Claudia became a bittersweet dream — a piece of forbidden fruit I should never have tasted. Oh, but for the pernicious class structure! Claudia had no idea what a good thing she was missing in Phillip Twersky.

That was when she started to phone me from abroad. She had been in Switzerland, doing whatever people did in Switzerland.

"I've been staying with Vlad, you know, Prince Todurescu? They're old friends of the family's. He's rather amusing — when he isn't being such a beast!"

All my work to get over her was for naught. I longed to be with her, doing whatever one did in Switzerland: bringing her chocolates, cleaning off her Swiss Army knife, winding up the cuckoo clock.

The next time she called, it was from London, where she was staying with her stepfather, Sir Lionel Spratling. "There's absolutely *nobody* in London these days," she said. "Why don't you come over, it would be amusing."

* * *

"Don't do it," said Malcolm, a few days later. "You can't follow her around the world like a puppy dog."

"That chick is trouble with a capital trouble," Malcolm's wife, Laura, added. "Besides, if you go to England you'll miss our cocktail party. You can meet some hot babes there!"

Hot babes, indeed. What did it matter when Plodgetts were in the offing? But Malcolm had a point — I couldn't just follow Claudia like a puppy dog. I had to have some excuse to go to London, but there I had a trick up my sleeve. My father's people were from London, originally from the East End slums but now safely removed to the North London suburb of Golders Green. Surely my family could come up with a wedding, bar mitzvah, or funeral. In my weekly telephone calls to my parents, I became especially solicitous of my British cousins.

"Yes, yes," my father would say. "Everyone's fine over there. What's come over you? It's almost as though you're expecting something to happen."

The weeks ticked by; Claudia kept calling. I told her I was too busy to go to London, what with all the fabulous cocktail parties one had to attend in Manhattan.

"Liar, liar, pants on fire," she said.

At last I broke down. The following Saturday, I told Claudia my Aunt Lucy had taken gravely ill, and I was going to visit her "in hospital," as we say in London. Perhaps I could squeeze Claudia into my busy schedule.

"Oh goody," she said.

The next challenge, of course, was explaining to my

Elated By Details

father why I was going to London without visiting any of his family. But then — wouldn't you know it — my father called with bad news.

"I just got off the phone with Uncle Frank in London," he said. "Your Granny's had a nasty fall. I'm afraid she's rather badly hurt."

"Oh, thank God!"

"What?"

"I mean, thank God she wasn't killed or anything."

"Yes, of course," my father said. "But she's going to be confined to her house for several weeks which can be very demoralizing at that age. You might just send her some flowers and a card."

"I can do better than that," I said. "How about if I go visit her?"

"That would be most thoughtful of you, Phillip."

* * *

I flew into Heathrow and took a taxi into the heart of swankest Mayfair, where I found myself ringing the bell of Sir Lionel Spratling's townhouse. Claudia answered.

"Wrong door," she said.

Claudia brought me in through the servant's entry, but we could not avoid running into Sir Lionel. After the briefest of introductions he excused himself, seemingly embarrassed at having been discovered in his own house. He glanced down at the stack of mail he was bringing in from the front hall, as if to explain his pressing need to review the correspondence. "One does get the most ferocious amount of bumf," he said.

"Me too," I said. "Especially from those public swimming pools."

Claudia glared at me, but I was not to be cowed. I was half British on the Twersky side and I had every right to be there. Besides, Sir Lionel would come to enjoy having such a wag for a step-son-in-law.

Even after Sir Lionel left for the country, the townhouse was crowded. Claudia's half-brother Massimo — Sir Lionel's son from a previous marriage to an Italian Contessa — kept trying to practice his English on me. He was having a hard time with "Fitzhugh."

"Fitz who?" he was saying.

"I give up," I answered.

Claudia insisted we check into a hotel where one might have privacy. One agreed. And for a couple of precious nights, one was finally alone with one.

* * *

The big mistake was bringing Claudia to my grandmother's house. Of course, *I* was obliged to go, having promised as much to my father. But I also had the notion, if Claudia could see me going so far out of my way to comfort a sick relation, it might fill that missing part of my personality — namely, my apparent inability to "drop every-

Elated By Details

thing" in the name of something greater than myself. It was what I had come to call my "passion gap." This visit would entail compassion, which, naturally, included passion.

I knew I'd forgotten something vital when Claudia asked, "Why are we going to your grandmother's house, when you said it was your Aunt Lucy who was sick?"

"Oh. Well. When I say 'granny' I mean 'Aunt Lucy.'"

"Why, pray tell?"

"It's one of those generational things," I said, holding an umbrella over Claudia. We were now standing on the doorstep of my Granny's semi-detached villa in Golders Green. "She's so much older than my father, we all just started calling her Granny. Crazy, huh?"

"Let's get out of the rain, shall we?"

"Granny!" I called out, making sure to wink at Claudia as I did. "You who!"

"Who you?" she cried back. "Oh, little Phillip! Cor' what a lot of noise you make. Wipe those boots off. There's a good boy. Don't want mud all over the nice clean 'ouse."

The house had that vaguely institutional smell of British middle class homes — the constant application of industrial cleanser being a popular means of staving off depression. I instinctively knew the smell would mean trouble with Claudia. I turned around to see her frozen in the hallway. She was wearing an Aquascutum raincoat, Hermés scarf, cream-colored cashmere sweater, and a long burgundy skirt. She was standing, her arms pressed rigidly against her sides, as if to keep from touching anything. I almost felt sorry for her.

At length, I coaxed Claudia into the sitting room where Granny was propped up in an easy chair, her feet resting on an ottoman and a blanket over her legs. "It's very nice to meet you, Julia," said Granny who was slightly deaf, anyway. "'ave some coffee with me. There's a love. All I've got is instant."

I went into the kitchen to make coffee.

Claudia spluttered, "Ah, how lucky Phillip is to have a nice Auntie like you."

"That's Granny, not Auntie."

I leaned out of the kitchen, getting Claudia's attention by making a corkscrew motion next to my temple, to indicate my Aunt Lucy was insane.

"Would one like milk in one's coffee?" I asked Granny.

"Don't be daft! You know I take milk!"

Granny took a sip of the instant coffee, closed her eyes and leaned her head back in a rather theatrical portrayal of convalescence. "Now, Phillip," she said. "I do 'ave a surprise. When I 'eard that you was coming over, I got on the blower and told the family. They're all going to be 'ere by noon, and they're bringing a lovely lunch!"

"But Granny, one can't stay. One has prior engagements," I lied. Claudia was relieved.

"What are you on about with 'one' this and 'one' that? Trying to talk like Prince Charles, are we? Well, never you mind, just invite your friends over 'ere! There'll be more than enough food, there always is."

"But—"

Elated By Details

There was some commotion at the front door; shoes being wiped, umbrellas shaken, coats hung up. My father's family had arrived. A stout woman in her mid-fifties entered the sitting room.

"Oh, hello Aunt Lucy," I said, avoiding Claudia's look.

* * *

"Obviously," I said, some hours later, cutting through the stony silence of the taxi ride, "since we call Aunt Lucy 'Granny,' we had to start calling our Granny 'Aunt Lucy.' It's as simple as that, really."

"One's head is *literally* pounding," said Claudia. "Besides, how can your grandmother be younger than your aunt?"

"Well, obviously, she's not my real grandmother, but a step grandmother. I would have thought you knew all about stepparents," I said pointedly. I might just pull this one off, I thought. "My grandfather just happened to marry a younger woman."

"Your grandfather? Is that the one you kept calling Uncle Frank?"

* * *

One hated to leave at a time like that, but I had to get back to my firm, having used up my allotted vacation time. I flew back to New York, while Claudia, Massimo, and Vlad

Todurescu were going to hear opera at Bayreuth. My relationship with Claudia, after the Granny caper, entered a frosty spell. As I boarded the taxi bound for Heathrow, Claudia's farewell was hardly encouraging.

"One hopes one is glad one came."

"Of course one is. Isn't one glad one came?"

"Of course."

"Call me when you get back to New York."

"Phillip. Don't be so absurd."

I flew back in a state of depression, the lordship of Plodgett Manor slipping through my fingers. Back in New York, I rallied for a time, as I chastely waited for Claudia to return. But upon our reunion in New York, I knew our fling, for that was all it was to be, was over.

We met in the bar of a club to which Claudia belonged. The waiter set our drinks down and stood at attention as she signed the chit. I crossed and re-crossed my legs several times.

"How odd to see you again," said Claudia, lighting a cigarette. That was not one of her usual vices.

"Darling," I reached for her hand.

"Don't," she said, withdrawing hers. "Listen, blue eyes, don't you know that sometimes you do something during the summer, and it feels right. Then a few months later, you realize, in fact, it was all rather absurd?"

"You mean that seersucker suit I bought?"

"Please, Phillip, don't make this more difficult for me. Things have changed; I'm with Vlad now."

Elated By Details

"Ah, the impaler."

"Don't be wicked."

"Sorry."

"Forget all that, Phillip. Let's be friends forever and ever, okay? Promise me."

"Okay," I said. Like, whatever.

"Drink your whisky, Phillip, and tell me what you're up to."

This presented an odd challenge. Now that our relationship was over, I was tempted to tell her the truth — that I'd been doing nothing but practicing law, going to the occasional movie, and eating mid-priced meals in ersatz bistros. But for once I had actually prepared a "passion" to unveil so as to impress Claudia. After a moment's hesitation, I decided to go ahead with the charade. It was important she regret dumping me.

"I'm glad you asked," I said. "I've been obsessively following events in South America. It's my new passion!" I laid it on thick, adlibbing a good deal about Brazilian politics, Argentine cinema, Peruvian novels, and Chilean wine.

"That's wonderful!" she said. "You know, Plodgett's Canned Soup has a factory somewhere down there. I could talk to my cousins; probably get you some sort of office job. Wouldn't that be divine?"

"Well, my Spanish is more literary than business-oriented. I'm not sure how useful I'd be."

"Oh, you'll probably be dealing with Americans the whole time. Besides, everyone speaks dollar. I was there once and I had *no* problem making myself understood."

"I don't know much about soup."

"Don't be absurd! The important thing is that you understand the culture! Anybody can learn about soup, for heaven's sake. How many smart lawyers are there who are passionate about South America?"

"I suppose you're right."

In a month it was all arranged. I quit my law firm and joined the offices of Plodgett's Canned Soup in Plata, the tiny republic wedged into the interstices between Argentina and Brazil. Claudia gave me the name of an exiled European aristocrat who proposed my membership in the *Club Británico*.

I have kept in touch with Malcolm and Laura, and it was from them that I learned of Claudia's break-up with Vlad, about a year after I'd been in Plata. It took another six months for me to extricate myself from Plodgett's. And now, I find myself leaving the coffee shop on Madison and heading to Claudia's apartment.

* * *

It is 1:20 when I step into Claudia's place. She is radiant. I kiss her on both cheeks and accept the sherry that is offered. Shades of Plodgett Manor?

"My cousins were so sorry to see you leave Plata," Claudia says. "And Tomás tells me the *Club Británico* will never be the same."

Elated By Details

"I think I got a ferocious amount of bumf there."

Claudia laughs.

"I was sorry to hear about you and Todurescu."

"Liar." She smiles. "Forget about that. I have an invitation for you."

"I accept. What is it?"

"My wedding."

"Oh."

"It's all incredibly sudden. I was with Jimmy Arbuckle, whom I hadn't seen in years, at Newport and he just popped the question. Can you believe it?"

"No."

"He's a lovely man, Phillip. You'll like him."

"Did he answer your question?"

"What question?"

"You know, Claudia, the one where you ask: what would make you drop everything and race across town? Did he answer that one?"

"Oh, yes. He had the right answer to that one."

"For God's sake, I've been struggling with that for years! Tell me, what did he say?"

"That's an easy one, Phillip. He just looked at me and said 'you.'"

THE BED

At some point in the middle of the George Washington Bridge, he wasn't sure whether he was in New Jersey or Manhattan, Nathan declared "I am not making a fool of myself." And then he looked in the rearview mirror to make absolutely sure nobody else was in the car.

He was just going to pick up a bed, that was all. It would be insanity to pay the extra delivery charge when he was perfectly capable of picking up the bed himself. He had a car, he had the time, and he needed to save money, now more than ever. He could have saved a lot more money by not buying a new bed in the first place, but that was a separate issue. "If you assume I need a new bed," Nathan said, summing up to a hypothetical jury, "the other arguments follow."

Elated By Details

The fact that Melissa would be at the furniture store was also a separate issue. If the practice of law had taught Nathan anything, it was how to keep separate issues separate. He had displayed that skill a week before, when he walked into the furniture store, found a saleswoman, and said: "I have three questions about four-poster beds."

"Well," replied the saleswoman, pretending to make a mental calculation, "that comes out to a twelve-poster question."

"Yes," Nathan said quickly. "Now, would you be the right person to ask those questions to?"

"Is that one of the three questions?"

"No," he said, and then realized she was joking. He smiled, shrugged, and nodded, his usual manner of acknowledging his leg was being pulled. It was only then Nathan registered that the saleswoman was pretty. That bothered him. It was a drag on the aerodynamics of the conversation. He forged ahead: "I guess I have four questions. One down and three to go. Ready for the other three?"

"Yes."

"One: do you carry four-poster beds? Two: if so, do you have any in a blond wood finish? And three: if the answer to the first two is yes, do you have any that are reasonably masculine in style?"

"I think the answer to all three questions is 'yes,'" she said.

"Fabulous," said Nathan. He had been skeptical when one of his colleagues at the law firm, a hip young partner named Paige, had told him to go to this place in Soho. It was called Expensive Crap, a self-parodically ironic emporium from the go-go 90's when new media entrepreneurs were on the lookout for "expensive crap" to fill their nearby lofts. Naturally, the prices had come down sharply since those days, but the management had decided to retain the original name. And so, the place remained "Expensive Crap," while carrying inexpensive crap — adding a whole new layer of irony to the package. And what was furniture without irony?

Nathan made his way down Riverside Drive. To his left, the Cathedral of St. John the Divine dominated the skyline with its enormous cross. It was just a couple of blocks from there, in a Columbia Law School classroom, that he had met Naomi, who had also, come to think of it, been enormously cross. Back then, her anger had been directed mainly at fascist professors, incompetent administrators, and conservative Supreme Court decisions. Nathan and Naomi very often found themselves on the same side of the law students' lunchroom debates. That's probably why she had asked him out.

"Excuse me, but what's your name," Nathan finally asked the saleswoman. She really was quite attractive.

"Melissa. Melissa Brighton. I'm usually here on weekends."

"Only on weekends?" said Nathan. The thought that she didn't have to work during the week depressed him. It meant she was "kept" by somebody, or she was still a student. He wanted her to be something else, something closer

Elated By Details

to a comrade in arms.

"Yeah," she said. "During the week, I do freelance work for a couple of interior design firms." And then she looked left and right with a conspiratorial air, "but I'm really hoping to break into retail full-time."

"Oh. Oh, I get it. That's a joke, right? You're an aspiring designer, right?"

"That's right, Mr—?"

"Nathan. Call me Nathan, obviously."

"What an unusual name."

Further down Riverside Drive, Nathan could now recognize the outskirts of the neighborhood where he and Naomi had moved after they were married. He remembered the wedding in mainline Philadelphia, near where her father taught college. It was an ultra-reform ceremony, as Naomi had wanted. Neither Naomi nor the rabbi appreciated Nathan's suggestion that they offer communion at the end of the thing, just for good measure.

When Nathan and Naomi moved into their Upper West Side apartment, with its radio permanently tuned to NPR and its coffee table laden with the *New York Times*, *New Yorker*, and *New Republic*, how cool were they? And prosperous, too. With both of them landing jobs at high-powered law firms, they aspired to a life of bourgeois bohemianism.

For a year or so, they worked like mad at their respective firms and enjoyed the affection that springs up between spouses who lead essentially separate lives. In the meantime, Naomi's anger — the third partner in the marriage — became unpredictable. The old targets of law school no longer mattered to her. The anger flitted around, sometimes landing on her colleagues from work, sometimes on the neighbors. When Nathan saw the anger coming, he tried to get out of the way, but that grew increasingly difficult.

Naomi hated the idea of a "family" without children; and then she blamed Nathan's carelessness when she got pregnant. With motherhood, Naomi took to railing against the patriarchal society that had saddled her with such heavy responsibilities. Nathan tried to make them all happier by getting them out of their suddenly cramped apartment and into a roomy suburban house. Naomi hated that, too.

"Have a nice day at work," she said one morning, "while I'm stuck in this fucking suburban ghetto!"

"There's really no need to yell," he said. And he thought: *couldn't you have said something before I took a half-million dollar mortgage*?

In the summers, he had allowed himself one precious week of vacation. Any more might jeopardize his partnership potential. He took the family to Martha's Vineyard. Little Julia scooped up sand in her fingers while Naomi looked angrily at all the unfamiliar faces. "Every fucking person we know is in the Hamptons," she said.

Melissa led Nathan to the bedroom displays. "We don't get a lot of requests for masculine four-poster beds," she said. "May I ask what inspired you?"

"I'm not sure," said Nathan. "It's just a picture I've had

Elated By Details

in my mind for a long time." Not even Nathan could remember where it came from. It may have been an old movie, or a cartoon, or even a dream. Somewhere along the line, the image of a four-poster bed had become a comfort to him. It was the kind of bed that ought to bring a couple closer together, a little roof under their roof, a touch of romance in their daily lives. Well, Naomi had scoffed at the suggestion, dismissing it as bourgeois without being the least bohemian.

Nathan walked beside her on the showroom floor. "Anyway, that's what I want and let's just say I've suddenly come into an unexpected degree of, er, *autonomy* in my home decorating choices." He directed a self-consciously bitter laugh in Melissa's direction. Autonomy was one way to put it. Six months ago, he and Naomi reached an impasse. All of their attempts at marriage counseling had only served to emphasize one fact: the only thing that they didn't like about the marriage was each other. Naomi asked for a separation. He left quietly. What was he going to do, start a fight in front of Julia?

Melissa knew better than to probe her customer about the "autonomy" thing. Instead, she led him to a heavy maple bed. "Here's one you might like," she said. "It's not exactly masculine, but it's quite simple and angular."

Nathan started walking around the bed. "Do you like it?" Melissa asked when Nathan was on his third lap.

"Yeah, I do. What do you call this style?"

"It's from an original by the Shakers."

"The Shakers?"

"They were involved with the Movers."

Nathan laughed. Melissa was shockingly attractive.

Despite her better instincts, Melissa allowed herself to think of Nathan as a man, rather than just a customer. She had never seen anyone trying so hard to be earnest and businesslike. The pain just below the surface was almost irresistible. Uh-oh, she thought, am I one of those women who loves too much?

"Wait, what's the time?" Nathan said abruptly, and then looked at his own watch. "Jesus, I've got a meeting at 3 o'clock."

"On a Saturday?" said Melissa.

"It's with the Movers," Nathan said. In reality, it was an appointment with his analyst.

"Better Shaker leg."

That was a week ago. Now Nathan was approaching Midtown, along the West Side Highway. He could see the slant-roofed tower where Naomi's firm had its offices. She had gone back to work part-time since the separation. She might be in the office now. For all Nathan knew, she might be flirting with a colleague. Nathan was alone in the car. His analyst had said he should try to work through his anger. He screamed in the general direction of Naomi's office: "You fucking bitch!" And then he felt ashamed, for he hardly ever raised his voice.

After six months of separation, there was no reconciliation in sight. He was right to start decorating his bachelor

Elated By Details

apartment. In fact, it was a miracle he'd kept his sanity in the cheerless one-bedroom flat for so long. Today, a bed. Tomorrow? Who knows — drapes?

A week ago, Nathan had hurried out of Expensive Crap to get to his analyst's office. After the appointment — at which it was decided Nathan was making good progress in dealing with the separation — he drove back to his apartment in New Jersey. That was when he started thinking about Melissa. Why the hell shouldn't he ask her on a date? True, the separation was only six months old, but it had been more like nine months since he and his wife had "made love" within the letter of that phrase — much longer within the spirit. On Sunday, he called Melissa at the shop.

"This is Melissa," she said.

Nathan had three questions: One: could he pick up the bed next Saturday? Two: if so, would she be there? And three: if so, would she like to go get a cup of coffee or something with him? He was breathing heavily. He hoped he didn't sound like a pervert. Was he making a gigantic fool out of himself?

But Melissa's answers to all three questions were satisfactory, even if a little tentative-sounding. Nathan spent the rest of the week in high spirits; getting a haircut, working out, preparing himself.

Now Nathan was steering his car through downtown Manhattan. He parked near Expensive Crap, checked himself in the mirror, brushed off his blazer, and sauntered into the store looking nervous as all hell. Melissa wasn't there.

The guy behind the register pulled out an envelope. "Are you Nathan? Melissa left this for you." He took the envelope, which was addressed to "Nathan Obviously." The note explained, in terms that seemed plausible, an emergency had come up with one of her freelance clients requiring her to work through the weekend. She didn't have Nathan's number, nor did Directory Assistance have any listing for a Nathan, Obviously.

The note ended with three questions. One: were you asking me on a date? Two: if so, are you a decent guy? Three: if so, why don't we do something fun, like go to a play? She left her home number.

THE MAGIC KINGDOM

Carla was fascinated by me. That much is fair to say.

"Do you have a background in acting, or performance of some kind?" The sputtering light of an aromatic candle — peaches 'n cream, I think it was — added an extra dash of mystery to the scene. Carla's eyes were wide with unfeigned interest. Eyes that reminded me of Gloria, whom I may or may not have seen the other day.

"Not at all," I said.

"But how did you end up in," she smiled, "this gig you've got?"

"I don't want to bore you," I said and let my voice trail off as I poured her another glass of the fine, fruity Italian number I'd picked up from the liquor store. Anyway, the trick worked. Carla protested that she *did* want to hear my story. I twirled my glass in the manner of a connoisseur, inhaling the perfume of the wine as though savoring the memories of a life well lived.

"Believe it or not," I said to Carla, "I used to work for a software company, selling products to small business. That is, until this one day about three months ago. As it happens, the day started off badly. Traffic was backed up on the Long Island Expressway and I got to the company late. I don't like being late. You spend the whole day feeling like you're on probation. Somebody's Volvo had taken my usual parking place, so I had to deposit my car in a remote corner of the lot.

"My cubicle was in a state of considerable disarray. The cleaning lady had evidently been taking out her aggressions on my workspace, even knocking over the little nameplate — a gift from Gloria — with its calligraphed "Alvin J. Puffin." I was still trying to establish a modicum of order on my desk when Jeff, a co-worker, said I really 'shouldn't bother' about the desk so much. That was the kind of attitude I had to combat daily at that job: why clean your desk when you could be closing yet another sale?

"It's true what they say about office jobs. They crush the soul, they squeeze the life out of you until your every move, every action, every preference and personal attribute is directed toward the bottom line." I wasn't just saying that to impress Carla. There *is* more to life than closing a sale. Every once in a while you do have to take time to clean your desk, or have a leisurely lunch, or sneak out of the office for

Elated By Details

a matinee or baseball game even though you've been repeatedly reprimanded for absenteeism. That kind of thing.

Carla was drinking it in. "Sounds like a genuine case of existential angst," she observed. Carla was a college senior and she used words like *angst*, which kind of turned me on. She brought me back to my early days with Gloria, when we were both undergraduates at St. John's and, believe me, the *bon mots* flew fast and furious. I knew they were *bon mots* because Gloria had a minor in French and she knew such things. We both had roommates back then, so there was a good deal of sneaking around and frustrated sofa-groping. But those days — autumn leaves, football games, parties, my arm around my sweetheart — they were magic.

"It was the day I usually gave my report to Mr. Franklin — to get back to the story — the head of my division. His secretary, a crusty old Irish woman, stopped me from going in, saying I lacked an appointment. This was obviously some new strategy of her own devising, since I had never required an appointment in the past. I was doubly annoyed, since my report was particularly good that day. I had even stayed up late the night before until my — then — wife, Gloria, more or less ordered me to bed.

"'Mr. Franklin will not be available all day,' the secretary said firmly. 'Now go away before I call building security.' What a flair for dramatics these Irish have! I almost told her to stop talking such a load of 'blarney,' but I decided to come back after she'd had her coffee, or tea, or whiskey, or whatever it was that made her human. I figured

Mr. Franklin would be asking after me soon enough.

"Next, I went to accounting, where I handed the clerk some receipts for my recent expenses. The clerk jabbed a few code numbers into the computer and told me, in a reedy, nervous voice, that the expenses were 'not authorized.' I could hardly believe it. I mean, there I was standing before him, flesh and blood, and he was obeying his computer rather than the evidence of his senses. What had we become? I was more than a collection of code numbers; my life was not a footnote to the office manual! I went on in that vein until the clerk summoned his supervisor.

"Oh, it's you Puffin," said Krauss, the supervisor, emerging from the safety of his large, but windowless, office. "You can't get these expenses reimbursed," he said with a weary sense of responsibility.

"What is this?" I asked Krauss." Was I now supposed to pay business expenses out of my own pocket? Was it not enough to sacrifice the best years of my life to the company? Would I now have to subsidize my own descent into the bowels of corporate America?

"Wow," said Carla. "What did Krauss say?"

"Oh well," I said, knocking off the last of the wine, for this was a delicate part of the story. "He just gave me some blather about how the expenses had been incurred after I was 'let go,' and so I said—"

"Let go?" said Carla. "What? You mean you'd been fired?"

"Well, I wouldn't say 'fired.'" I made little quotation

Elated By Details

marks in the air, indicating my distaste for the word. "Besides, technically, it takes a few days for the paperwork."

"But you *knew* you'd already been 'let go?'"

I admitted as much.

Carla was shaking her head. "And you — you stayed up late writing a report for this Mr. Franklin?" Her voice was twisting upward like a corkscrew. "And you cleaned up your desk? And submitted expense reports? Why?"

I had been afraid of this reaction. "Please, let me finish the story," I said.

"Let me guess," said Carla, reaching for her handbag, "this is the part where you pull out the AK-47 and mow down a dozen innocent co-workers?"

"Oh dear! Have I told you this one already?" I cried, trying to make a big joke out of the whole thing.

"Look Alvin, it's late." She stood up.

"Just a few more minutes," I pleaded.

For the rest of the story, I allowed Carla to position herself near the front door. This involved no great maneuvers, for I live in a very small efficiency apartment. In any event, as I explained to Carla, I guess you could say I was in denial. "It is, after all, a textbook reaction to any shock and getting fired certainly had been a shock. But it wasn't just that I couldn't admit the truth to myself; I couldn't admit it to my wife.

"You see, there had been trouble in paradise, as they say, for some months now. Even though Gloria and I had been college sweethearts, living as man and wife turned out to be totally different from dating. I mean, Gloria had become terribly judgmental. Nothing I did was any good. I left for work too late or I came home too early. I spent my weekends with my nose in a book instead of cleaning up the condo, or doing the laundry, or taking her into the City for dinner and a show, or any one of the mutually exclusive things she wanted me to do all at once. Without any warning, her mood would sometimes shift and she would demand we start having children — which I wasn't going to do with our relationship on the rocks, thank you very much.

"How could I tell Gloria I'd been fired? It would be the ultimate 'I told you so,' the conclusive proof of my worthlessness. After my run-in with the accounting department, I got into my car and started driving down back roads with no particular direction. I kept hearing Gloria's voice in my head: 'Well Alvin, what are you going to do now? What are you going to do now?'

"This imaginary conversation brought to mind a series of ads that ran on TV a few years back. Perhaps you remember them? They featured supposedly impromptu interviews with people who had achieved great fortune. In each ad, the interviewer would say something like, 'Hey, Joe Blow, you just won the lottery. What are you going to do now?' To which, Joe Blow would answer, 'I'm going to Disneyworld!'

"So that's when I decided to go to Disneyworld." Carla put her hand on the doorknob at this point. "I had a nice

Elated By Details

drive down the coast. I even called Gloria from Philadelphia to let her know I was taking a little vacation. But she launched into such an irrational tirade, I had to hang up on her. And within a few days, I arrived."

"I should really get going," Carla said, opening the door. "Thanks for dinner."

"But—"

She was gone. Not that I blame her; I know my story sounds a little weird. And I'll be the first to admit that my original reasons for going to Disneyworld were a little sketchy. But the thing is — which I would have explained to Carla had she given me the chance — that once I arrived at Disneyworld, the whole trip took on a new meaning. Life is like that sometimes. You do things by pure instinct — turning down a side street, ordering a new dish, buying a book with a nice cover, only to find out that your actions, in retrospect, made perfect sense.

Disneyworld exemplified those mysterious workings of life. My parents had never taken me there and so the place was a total revelation to me. It was full of the things we seem to have lost in the working world: a sense of joy, wonder, play, safety, and cleanliness. During the first few days, I knocked around Epcot, Universal Studios, and all the rest, calling Gloria several times a day. I knew, if she would only join me down here, it would give our relationship a new lease. Couples need that. They need a framework, a certain set of shared memories that form their secret myth. With Gloria and me, our college days were fading into the past;

we needed a new start, namely, Disneyworld.

Gloria wasn't buying it. She started screening her calls and eventually switched to an unlisted number. After a couple weeks, she had my ATM card and credit cards frozen. I checked out of the motel and spent a very uncomfortable night in the Hyundai. But the next morning, I still wanted to stay near Disneyworld! That was when I marched right up to the Disneyworld Office of Personnel and asked what jobs they had available *immediately* for somebody with no relevant experience, no references, and no permanent address. I was referred to a Mr. Crumble, an older man with a beard and habit of sucking on breath mints all day.

Mr. Crumble was quite forthright in telling me that jobs were not ordinarily available for the picking, "like ripe peaches from the tree," to use his colorful phrase. "However," he said, looking me over, "you might be tall enough for Goofy." It seems that one of their Goofies had quit without any advance notice, leaving them in a fix, Goofy-wise. Well, the costume fit and so I began my career of delighting young and old alike as an official Goofy in the Magic Kingdom portion of Disneyworld.

Don't get me wrong. My ego took a hit. I had been a salesman for one of the leading software distributors in the Northeast. Now I was wearing a Goofy costume. These transitions take their toll. Most of my time was spent in the company of toddlers, who are prone to pee in their pants and/or vomit in the presence of larger-than-life cartoon characters. But the job did allow me to move out of my car

Elated By Details

and get an efficiency apartment. I was even able to buy a few furnishings, on credit, from the employee store. Everything is decorated with Disney characters, but it kind of grows on you.

I worked hard at the job and never complained, despite the oppressive heat of that damn costume. Mr. Crumble was clearly relieved he had been right to take a chance on me and he began to regard me as his protégé. I took to stopping by the personnel office to have a chat with Crumble and, incidentally, to see if any new "opportunities" had come up. That was how I met Carla, who was doing some kind of work-study thing to complement her business degree at Florida State. I told Carla about my life as a Goofy in lurid surrealist tones that seemed to amuse her.

My date with Carla; that is, the date I was describing just a minute ago, was not a great success. But then, it was my first date since Gloria had asked for a divorce and I still needed to refine my pitch. The facts of life are given; what really defines us is how we tell the tale. I thought a lot about how to tell the story of my young life, for the purposes of my next date, or my next friend, or whatever. Thinking about the past inevitably leads one to thoughts about the future. It was like writing those reports for Mr. Franklin. I had to try to link up my past experiences with my future strategy.

One thing Carla said kept coming back to me: was I an actor? No, but maybe that's where all this was headed. After all, wasn't my brief career as a salesman akin to being an actor? And isn't being a Goofy a kind of performance, no matter how rudimentary? Fortunately, Disneyworld offers unparalleled opportunities for thespians of all levels. With Crumble's help, I was able to get a bit part providing background "color" in a 1940's New York street scene that plays more or less permanently in Disneyworld. I was supposed to strike up improvised conversations with passing tourists. What with my New York background, I was able to develop a pretty convincing shtick that pleased my supervisors no end.

Soon, I was landing more small parts in the never-ending cycle of productions that make Disneyworld such a delightful place. It was great fun, and it meant extra cash with which I was able to get some decent clothes for my after-work life. It was during a crowd scene in the abridged *Hunchback* that I found myself standing next to Lucy, an aspiring actress. Lucy had rather mousy hair, but the sweetest smile, and she knew how to wear a French peasant dress, if you know what I mean. During one of the breaks, I bought her a Diet Coke and made her laugh with my Quasimodo impression.

Lucy and I became an item. We lingered over coffee at the employee cafeteria, falling into those playful but passionate debates for which artists are famous. Lucy was a follower of Stella Adler, believing she could best realize her characters through abstraction, a kind of "pure" acting. I favored the more Strassbergian take on the Stanislavski "method," drawing on life experiences to inform my inter-

Elated By Details

pretation of Goofy as well as the other characters in my repertoire. During these debates, Lucy would repeat the old chestnut about Dustin Hoffman and Sir Laurence Olivier on the set of *Marathon Man*; the one that ends with Sir Laurence saying "why not try acting, my dear boy?" When Lucy delivered the punch line with a plummy English accent, we would collapse into giggles.

Am I in love with Lucy? No. But she does have a heart of gold. She makes no demands on me, and expresses gratitude when I treat her to a Diet Coke or a movie ticket. She knows when I need to brood — artists need brooding time. Sometimes I think Lucy is the only thing that has made my new life worth living. But we're not computers. We don't ingest data and spit out love. It has to happen naturally. I have settled into a routine with Lucy that is comfortable and satisfying, even though part of me yearns for some indefinable *je ne sais quoi*, as Gloria used to say.

Which brings me to the other day, when I may or may not have seen Gloria here at the Magic Kingdom. I say "may or may not" because I was on Goofy duty at the time, and the costume cuts down on one's peripheral vision rather severely. By the time I swiveled around to get a better look at her, some brat was tugging at my sleeve. When I looked up again, she was gone. The glimpse I caught looked like her — the auburn hair, the sensuous hips, a ghost of a smile on the three-quarter profile. And it would not be unusual to find Gloria in a place like Disneyworld. She worked as a travel agent and was constantly getting offered free promotional trips to resort places. She was also with a man, but whether it was a boyfriend or just her brother Jim, I couldn't tell.

I was haunted by the possible sighting of Gloria. She would know from my recent postcards — I hadn't stopped writing, even though she never wrote me, except through her lawyer — that I was still in Disneyworld. I wondered why she would come, except to find me. At other times, I was convinced the woman I saw was a perfect stranger, sharing only the most basic features with my soon-to-be ex.

Lucy noticed the change in me right away and started bugging me to take a vacation. Everyone needs a vacation, Lucy said, even from Disneyworld. Lucy seemed a little put out when I told her I was taking a vacation alone, but she came around like a trooper. It being October, things had slowed down enough for me to get a couple of weeks off, with Crumble's help.

I jumped into the old Hyundai and just started driving north a couple days ago. It was one of those life decisions I talked about a minute ago. No good reason, just a gut feeling. Once again, the logic of things became clear only after the fact. As I made my way up through Virginia, then Maryland, and Delaware, the autumn nip in the air and the blazing foliage told me I was doing the right thing.

Now, nursing my beer in the comfort of a motel room in King of Prussia, PA, I know I will go to Long Island. I will stop by Gloria's travel agency, maybe surprise her with flowers, and take her out for a nice lunch. Not romantic, but just as a gesture; a way of apologizing for the abrupt way I

Elated By Details

left. And maybe I'll be able to explain what a hard time I was going through that day I drove away; the way my self-esteem was at an all-time low, the way marriage and working suddenly crashed down around me like a prison sentence.

Maybe, just maybe, I'll be able to convince Gloria to take a road trip to St. John's to see the football game — there's one this weekend. We could put on our old sweatshirts and caps and maybe leave all the unpleasantness behind us. There is still time for reconciliation. I'll get an office job. Office jobs aren't so bad, in reality, and we could even start a family. It certainly isn't wrong for me to make one last attempt with Gloria. I mean, even if she still wants a divorce. "I wouldn't blame you," I'll say to her. At least we could end things on a positive note.

The last dregs of beer put me in a philosophical mood. Even if things don't go well with Gloria it won't be the end of the world. As long as I get back to Orlando in twelve days, I'll still have my job. With the weather cooling down, the Goofy costume will be more comfortable. There's certainly room to grow as an actor. And what the hell! I could end up on Broadway or in the movies. Then Gloria would be sorry! And, of course, Lucy will be waiting for me when I get back. This time, at least, I didn't burn my bridges. Who says people can't change?

JUSTICE AFTER A FASHION

"In a move still rare for local law firms, Cadwalader Wickersham & Taft announced March 6 that the dress code will be business casual all year round....Polo Ralph Lauren, along with *Esquire* magazine, are planning a fashion seminar for Cadwalader attorneys and staff in early April."
— *New York Law Journal*, March 24, 2000.

OFFICIAL TRANSCRIPT
State v. Parmenter
Supreme Court, New York County

Judge Stone: The Court will come to order. The prosecution has requested a continuance of two months. This is

Elated By Details

most irregular. Would you care to explain this request, Ms. Finkel?

Ms. Finkel: Your Honor, to hold the trial before the Carolina Herrera show would be a mockery of justice.

Judge Stone: I fail to see the relevance.

Ms. Finkel: The prosecution has evidence that cigarette pants and tulip skirts are going to be huge this season. I'm going to need time to shop.

Judge Stone: What does the defense say, Mr. Nolan?

Mr. Nolan: The defense objects! You don't see me asking for a continuance until after the Barney's warehouse sale, do you?

Judge Stone: Barney's?

Ms. Finkel: Oh please! Like this guy shops at Barney's? Your Honor, defense counsel is wearing a Land's End "business casual" shirt.

Mr. Nolan: Ms. Finkel is way out of line. This happens to be a Thomas Pink shirt. Granted, it's Green Label, not Black Label, but let the record reflect that the Green Label features the same high quality tailoring as Black Label, but with unstructured collars and bold Havana checks.

Ms. Finkel: For the record, Mr. Nolan's shirt is, at best, from Brooks Brothers, which makes me think: what is he? Is he a traditionalist like the "old" Brooks Brothers, or is trying to be hip like the "new" Brooks Brothers.

Judge Stone: Counselor, I think we're digressing.

Ms. Finkel: With all due respect, Your Honor, that is easy for you to say. You've got that head-to-toe black number that is just so eternally chic. And slimming, too.

Judge Stone: Are you laughing, counselor?

Mr. Nolan: I'm sorry, Your Honor, I thought that was kind of a good one.

Judge Stone: Is that so? Well, maybe I'll just grant Ms. Finkel's continuance, then.

Mr. Nolan: The defense objects to any trial during a transitional season. It is basically impossible to find good outfits in those "in-between" weights. You know what I mean?

Ms. Finkel: The prosecution submits Exhibit A: a Paul Stuart catalog clearly showing a lightweight silk/cashmere crewneck that defense counsel would look, well, terrific in.

Mr. Nolan: (Whispering) You really think so?

Ms. Finkel: (Whispering) Definitely.

Judge Stone: Hello? I'm denying the continuance. Any questions?

Ms. Finkel: Yes. Where am I supposed to find outfits that are wrinkle-free, bold, and yet not too frivolous for the jury?

Mr. Nolan: In *State v. Johnson*, the prosecution did just fine with a sheath dress in basic colors that she was able to brighten up with accessories.

Ms. Finkel: I don't know, Your Honor, don't you think some prints would be nice?

Judge Stone: The Court takes no position whatsoever—

Mr. Nolan: It's going to be a lot easier for the prosecution to jazz up an outfit with accessories than tone down

Elated By Details

some wacky print. Granted, it may not be what Ms. Finkel wants for after work—

Ms. Finkel: It's not like I've been going out much after work lately, Mr. Nolan.

Mr. Nolan: Me neither. And please, call me John.

Ms. Finkel: Thanks. I'm Catherine.

Judge Stone: Okay, fine! I'm granting the continuance. Now go away. Both of you.

Mr. Nolan: This isn't fair. My client is languishing in jail.

Ms. Finkel: I might have agreed with that characterization back in the days of those old stripy uniforms. But today's penal system favors monochromatic separates in muted colors and loose fits. So, I wouldn't be shedding any tears over Mr. Nolan's client.

Mr. Nolan: It's not just the uniform. He hasn't exfoliated in weeks.

Ms. Finkel: Your Honor, his client is an embezzler!

Mr. Nolan: He only did it so that he could buy his wife six pairs of Manolo Blahniks.

Judge Stone: Mr. Nolan, are you admitting your client's guilt?

Mr. Nolan: Any decent man would do that for his wife.

Ms. Finkel: You really think so, John?

Mr. Nolan: Absolutely. *I* would, if I were married—

Judge Stone: In light of counsel's admission, I find the defendant guilty and sentence him to the maximum—

Ms. Finkel: Your Honor, the prosecution is dropping all

charges against that wonderful man.
    Mr. Nolan: Thanks, Catherine—
    Judge Stone: In all my years on the bench—
    Mr. Nolan: And if I may so say, that belted jacket is so 70's redux, I could just scream.
    Judge Stone: Let's go off the record.
    Ms. Finkel: But never off the rack!
    Mr. Nolan: Well said, Catherine. Lunch?
    Ms. Finkel: Why not?
    Judge Stone: Case dismissed.

THE EDUCATION OF
ANDREW PEARLSTEIN

Looking back, it's hard to believe I once ran through the rain to get to Latin class. But it was the fall of my freshman year and I had the idea that collecting some truly Dickensian memories would be a comfort to me in my dotage.

Mother Nature was doing her best to oblige. A cold New England rain fell across Old Campus; it came down in sheets in the manner usually achieved only on Hollywood sets. I sprinted along a flagstone path, grunting out the morning lesson, trying to make each syllable coincide with my footfalls:

Hic, haec, hoc,
Huius, huius, huius—

That I had freely chosen to take a morning Latin class was a mystery even to me. It had something to do with elevating myself, making myself worthy of this ancient institution. The gargoyles and spires of Old Campus mocked me that morning for the green Midwesterner I was. I answered back in my defiant Pig Latin: *ix-nay on the ock-may*!

I reached the classroom in the odd state of being both cold and sweaty. I stood outside the door, catching my breath and listening to the drone of Professor Hayduck's voice. Opening the door produced, as seemed only fitting, a piercing squeal from the hinges. All eyes turned to me.

"Sorry I'm late."

"Not at all," Professor Hayduck said with bland malice. "In fact, I owe you an apology. I must get those hinges oiled."

There was scattered laughter from the students. I settled into a chair at the back, directly behind Zoë Wapping. Zoë was from Boston and was taking Latin "with a definite view to majoring in Classics." I was taking Latin with a definite view to Zoë Wapping's neck. She possessed a neck I cherished; a neck I wanted to take back to my room with me. I would send for the rest of the body later.

Yes, part of me wanted a bleak Dickensian existence; but another part craved a life saturated with erotic adventures. I had arrived at college a virgin, my high school years stymied by an inability to engage in sex, or any other vice, while in the same time zone as my parents. Now that I was on Eastern Standard Time, my battle cry was "experience":

Elated By Details

accumulated experience; hoarded experience; experience that could be traded in for wisdom when at last I knew the proper exchange rate.

After a minute or two, the classroom door squealed again. It was Isaac. Tall and skinny, carrying an umbrella that was the same, he brushed a few droplets off of his army surplus greatcoat.

Professor Hayduck cocked his head in silent inquiry.

"Sorry," said Isaac. "There was a fire at the soup kitchen — had to deal with it." The professor sighed heavily, but resisted the urge to sarcasm. Soup kitchens were in particularly high esteem during those early years of the Reagan administration. As Isaac settled into the chair next to mine, some wag muttered: "That guy has awesome excuses." Isaac, who had never before spoken to me, looked at me and winked.

I felt strangely blessed by Isaac's acknowledgment. After all, he had been putting out fires at the soup kitchen while I had merely overslept because my roommate, John Waddington, and I had been up until three in the morning with one of our freshman year where-do-you-draw-the-line conversations.

"... corporibus," Professor Hayduck was saying. "What case is that? Pearlstein? *Mister* Pearlstein?"

"Umm," I intoned, as though warming up for my part in a barbershop quartet. I flipped through the text, hoping the right answer would jump out at me. "Let's see. I think it's— I think—"

"Attic?" the professor suggested.

"That's it!"

"I'm afraid not," said Hayduck, grinning. "Attic doesn't exist in Latin. Only in Greek."

"Bastard," said Isaac, 40 minutes later, and a safe distance from Professor Hayduck. Still, I appreciated the gesture of solidarity. We were walking toward Freshman Commons, where lunch would be served. We drifted into the cafeteria with the unspoken clicking of playground friendships. Isaac kept on with his rant against Hayduck throughout lunch. "He's just bitter because he got passed over for tenure at Williams."

How did he know such things? "Yeah," I said. *Insouciant* had been one of the SAT words I learned in my junior year of high school, and it was a quality to which I had aspired ever since. I said that "yeah" with as much insouciance as I could muster.

"Where are you from?" Isaac asked.

"Chicago. Well, suburbs, technically. And you?"

"New York," he said, with as much insouciance as *he* could muster, which was a lot more than I could.

After lunch, Isaac announced he was off to see his brother.

"Your brother's here?"

"Yeah, he's a junior," said Isaac, matter-of-factly. Boy, was he winning this insouciance game. "He's starting up a new magazine," he said, still referring to his brother. "Fiction, non-fiction, poetry, science, everything. It's going

Elated By Details

to be called *Erasmus*. You should get involved."

I had no burning desire to write, but I wanted to do whatever Isaac and his invisible brother were doing, so I joined the "staff" of *Erasmus*. For the inaugural issue, I contributed an essay about the campus movement for a nuclear freeze, which I endorsed with freshman passion. Isaac composed a poem. At our first editorial meeting, Isaac proudly displayed me to his brother, Simon, introducing me as a Midwestern Jew who studied Latin. "We're, like, both on Hayduck's shit list," Isaac said, relishing every word.

"Hayduck!" groaned Simon, and we all had a good laugh at this private joke, the punch line of which was evidently "Hayduck."

Simon honored Isaac and me, not only by printing our drivel, but also by allowing us to deliver the magazine to all the pigeon holes on Old Campus. It was carrying around bundles of *Erasmus* that cemented our friendship, amidst a good deal of Latin hilarity — "Hand me an *Erasmus* — oops, make that two *Erasmi*!"

I took insouciance lessons from Isaac. Simon even treated us to lunch at the upperclassmen's dining club, where we slurped down raw oysters in the manner dictated by *Brideshead Revisited*, which was then showing on PBS. Somewhere along the line, Isaac confessed that he had stopped going to the soup kitchen. "I guess I'd better be on time for Hayduck now," he said rather sheepishly.

November rolled around. John Waddington and I continued our late-night, line-drawing exercises; distinguishing

—or not— between abortion and the death penalty; censorship and community standards; sanctions against China and those against South Africa; the lyrics of Elvis Costello and the poetry of William Blake. What I lacked in intellect, I tried to make up for in witticisms. "I do favor the death penalty — for suicide." The leaves fell on schedule and I discretely ditched the clothes of suburban Chicago for the dark thrift store togs I thought appropriate to my new station.

There remained the problem of sex; an abstraction made flesh by Zoë Wapping and her neck. One evening I saw her at a reading; somebody was declaiming an updated translation of the *Aeneid*. "I sing of man and handgun violence" was the new opening line. After the reading, I suggested to Zoë, polishing off the old insouciance, that we "grab a cup of coffee."

"Sure," she said.

I was temporarily speechless, paralyzed by my freshman superstition that going for coffee with girls was invariably a prelude to sex. "Let's go to Beth's," Zoë said, breaking the silence.

We went to said Beth's, which was a coffee bar favored by the bohemian set. Inside, the smell of organic coffee and clove cigarettes mingled with the sounds of modern jazz and earnest conversations, all of which involved the word *Salvador* — Allende, Dali, El. Zoë was a great mystery: the sandy blond hair piled up in back, the clothes that managed to be loose, androgynous, and still to give some hint of the mysteries underneath. She was also maddeningly unim-

Elated By Details

pressed by my bold stand in favor of a nuclear freeze. Politics held no interest for her.

I tried to whip up a froth of controversy. "Don't you care that Reagan is trying to get rid of public broadcasting, and public universities, and stuff like that?"

"I used to be apathetic," she said, "but then I just couldn't be bothered."

Two could play at that game. "Me, I'm growing bored of apathy."

And so began a veritable Algonquin Round Table, somewhat complicated by my attempts to work in a theme of "beautiful necks in Western Culture" such as the one on Bernini's Saint Theresa — which I had studied in Art History, hoping Zoë would get the idea. Instead, all she told me was that so-called Western art was hopelessly patriarchal. As she got up to pay the bill, I blurted out: "There's a keg party at Durfee on Saturday night. Wanna go?"

"Keg party?" she gave a sideways smile. "That's not really my scene."

"Well, would you like to have dinner sometime?" Please God, kill me now.

"Maybe," she said. "But I'm pretty busy for the next couple of weeks."

I played the closest thing to a trump card I possessed. "Because I was just wondering; I thought we could talk about this new magazine, *Erasmus*. I'm, like, on the staff."

"Oh that's Isaac's thing, isn't it?"

"And his brother, Simon," I said.

"They're such Horace Mann boys," she said. Reading the confusion on my face, Zoë explained: "That's the prep school they went to in the City. They're all a little slick for me."

I didn't know whether to defend the Glockenspiels — that was Isaac and Simon's last name — or continue the chase. I decided the Glockenspiels could look after themselves. "Well, it's a good magazine. You should really write something — you know, about Western art being patriotic."

"That's *patriarchal*."

"Yeah. You should do that for the next issue."

"What's the hurry?"

"Who knows? Reagan might get rid of it."

I did manage to get Zoë to dinner one night. She had submitted something to *Erasmus*, a translation of some ancient love poem that I interpreted as a secret message to me. After dinner, I invited her to my room, having already arranged things with John, to "look over" her poem. As Roxy Music played on my cassette deck, I made my move with a clumsy, hungry lunge.

"No," she said, holding out her hand. "Andrew, no."

"Sorry! I just thought— I mean, I really like you."

"I like you, too, Andrew," she said, and she said it with such conviction, it almost seemed like an acceptable consolation prize. "It's too soon. I'm just starting college — you, too for that matter. I need to experiment more, figure out who I am. I'm not sure I believe in the whole conventional heterosexuality thing. Who knows? Like, maybe who I real-

Elated By Details

ly am is a lesbian? At least I want to experiment."

I was hurt and titillated in more or less equal measures. I tried to put a brave face on things by telling Zoë I understood. "What about that love poem you translated? Wasn't that sort of conventional?"

"It's Sappho, Andrew."

"I know," I said, and made a mental note to find out who or what Sappho was.

Zoë and I agreed to be friends. We went for walks through the quadrangles or study breaks at Beth's. She would cut the sexual tension between us by mocking the various campus "couples" one could see walking arm and arm, as though celebrating their diamond anniversary. "Don't you think we're all a little young to fall into the same old pattern of boy-girl, kissy-face, going all the way?"

"Could be fun," I suggested.

"The pleasure momentary, the position ridiculous, and the expense damnable," she said. "That's Oscar Wilde."

"And look where he ended up," I said. Oh, I was learning all right.

The major drama of semester's end was a beard-growing contest between John and myself, the results of which were still clinging to my face when Isaac invited me to New York for Christmas break. My parents were agreeable, provided I made an appearance in Chicago for at least a few days at the end of vacation.

The Sunday before Christmas, I arrived at the Glockenspiels. They had a big spread on Central Park West decorated with Futurist paintings and African sculptures. Isaac's father, Carl, was a big-shot international lawyer and an adjunct professor of human rights at NYU law school. I learned this, and more, the morning of my arrival. Carl was one of those people whose conversation consists of resume snippets. He asked where I "hailed from."

"Ah, the Windy City," he said when I told him. "I once tried a massive case in Chicago. I was stuck in the Four Seasons for a whole month—"

Isaac took me out to lunch at a little Cuban hole-in-the-wall after which we walked around the Upper West Side. This being my first time in Manhattan, I was still in the neck-craning, gee-whiz mode when Isaac muttered, "We should head back; my dad's wife will be home now."

Isaac had mentioned a "stepmother" some weeks ago, but the word conveyed nothing to me, since stepmothers were fairytale creatures in my mind. But "my dad's wife" — that phrase brought to mind After School Specials featuring tragedy, alienation, and Oedipal complications. It turned out that Isaac's parents had divorced when Isaac was seven. A few years ago, Carl had married one of his NYU students. Barbara was the name of Carl's wife — a woman whom Isaac regarded with a permanent sneer. Despite her law degree and her job at a small law firm, Carl considered Barbara to be a deeply unserious person. He called her various names behind her back, the most common being "Dad's bit of fluff."

The bit of fluff was there when we got back to the

Elated By Details

house. "Barbara," said Isaac, "I want you to meet my friend, Andrew."

Barbara looked to be in her late thirties, with a second wife's nervous smile. She was wearing slacks, a yellow silk blouse, and some bracelet that jangled. As I drew closer to shake her hand, my eyes grappled with the neckline of her blouse. She pretended not to notice. "So Andy," she said, lighting a cigarette. "Does your mother know about that beard?"

"Not exactly."

"Maybe we'd better do something about it before you go home."

"You think so?"

Barbara laughed. Carl cleared his throat. "I grew a beard when I was at Harvard Law School—"

Over the next few days, Isaac and I trawled the neighborhoods of Manhattan while keeping up a constant riff of College humor. "Ah, you're such a Horace Mann boy!" I would say. Most evenings, Carl would insist on "family dinners" which had the virtue, for him, of providing a captive audience. His autobiographical monologues were made bearable only by the generous supply of wine — which I was not used to drinking at all, let alone on a daily basis — and the regular interruptions of Barbara, whom I now inwardly referred to as Babs, a name bandied about during my fantasy romps with her. One evening, around Christmas, as Carl was describing an unworthy adversary in one of his legal cases, he worked himself up to a crescendo, saying

"That man was nothing but a whore for his client. I've never met anyone so meretricious!"

Babs raised her glass. "Meretricious and a Happy New Year!" There was polite laughter from everybody, except me who was doubled over in uncontrollable giggles. When I realized everyone was staring at me, I gasped "I'm sorry. I just—" between guffaws. I excused myself to go to the bathroom, and returned to Carl's brick-faced silence.

The next day, I tried to keep a low profile, being both hung-over and embarrassed about my performance at dinner. While Isaac went to try to get Knicks tickets from a scalper, I stayed inside. I was sitting in the Glockenspiel's handsome library, pretending to read some Eastern European novel when Babs came in.

"I brought you a present," she said brightly, plopping a small Bergdorf Goodman bag on the side table. It was full of high-priced shaving paraphernalia; a pearl-handled razor; French *crème a raser*; English aftershave. "If you're going to laugh at my jokes, I want to see your face properly," she said. "Besides, your poor mother will never forgive me if I send you home with that growth."

"Thanks."

"What are you waiting for?" she said. "Let's see that face."

Some time later, I emerged from the bathroom clean-shaven and presented myself to Babs. "Not bad," she declared. "It's a good face, you shouldn't have covered it up. But you've got razor burn, or freezer burn, or whatever

Elated By Details

they call it. Wait a sec." She ran off to the master bath and brought back some facial moisturizer Carl used.

"Sit down," she commanded, pointing to an ottoman. She squeezed some moisturizer into her hands and rubbed it on my cheeks in a firm, circular motion as I looked up at the undulating lines of her blouse. Then she kneeled behind me and, reaching around, slowly massaged the moisturizer into my neck. She smelled of shampoo and cigarettes.

Hic haec hoc; huius huius huius; Chicago, parents, Carl, anything, I said to myself, but there was nothing I could do to stop an erection. I hoped Babs didn't see, but she was kneeling right behind me. I heard a door open and then Isaac's voice call out, "Andrew, come on! I got the tickets!" I slumped in the ottoman feeling relief, disappointment, and a wave of fatigue. Babs tousled my hair. "You'd better go play with Isaac."

By the time we got back from the game, the elder Glockenspiels were in bed, so I had to content myself with such memories of Babs as I could conjure up. Those memories slowly dissolved into a lurid dream I enjoyed in reruns over the next few nights. At the family dinners, my eyes would occasionally meet Babs' in what I imagined to be a look of mutual understanding.

Just after the New Year, Carl went away on a business trip. "I should just buy a house in The Hague," he said as he left. I couldn't have agreed more. Given the antipathy between Isaac and the bit of fluff, there was no pretense of family dinners while Carl was away. I went to the movies with Isaac; Babs had dinner with a friend. We got back late and, after a brief raid on the liquor cabinet, Isaac went off to bed. I went to the library to read. Half an hour later, as I slept in a chair, *Eminent Victorians* covering most of my face, I heard a voice.

"Andy, Andy, Andy." It was Babs.

"Whummuflp?" I said rubbing my face. "Oh, it's you. Hi."

She was wearing a tee shirt and jeans, rather than the silk teddy of my fantasies, but the outfit, as they say, worked for me. Her hair was hanging loose about her shoulders and she was, or seemed to be, without makeup.

"Do you mind if I call you Andy? Or Handy Andy? Or Randy Andy?"

"How 'bout if I call you Babs?"

"Babs!" she laughed. "Well, I guess it's only fair. But let's just make that one of our little secrets." She was not wearing a bra. I wanted to spend the spring semester inside that tee shirt.

She sat down on the arm of my chair. "So, Andy, do you have a girlfriend at school?"

"No," I said.

"Too bad," she said, drawing her face a half-inch closer to mine. "School always used to make me horny."

"Really?" She put me out of my misery by pulling my face into hers. The next thing I knew she was sitting in my lap and the next thing after that, I was in the master bedroom. With her expert hands, and constant injunctions to

Elated By Details

keep my voice down, Babs guided me out of Virginity. I must have been a promising student, for the following night, I was allowed into the master bedroom for a repeat performance. I left for Chicago the next morning.

Pretty soon I was back at college, possessed of two personalities that were battling for supremacy. On the one hand, I felt myself to be a Big Man on Campus, a virile chest-thumping gorilla; ravisher of a genuine bit of fluff. On the other hand, I was a silenced eunuch, banished from the only coital bed I'd ever known. My only real confidant, Isaac, could not catch wind of the affair, and in any event, Babs had sworn me to secrecy. Worse, she had warned me that "this" could never happen again. But then, she had said that after the first night, and "this" happened again, the next night.

It slowly dawned on me that Babs and I had what people called an "unspoken understanding." I thought of the way she had awakened me in the early hours of that first morning "Well, you *are* Randy Andy." Could life possibly hold anything more profound than the depths of our mutual desire? She was the princess in the castle, trapped in a loveless marriage with the grim Carl. Naturally, she had told me to keep my distance. That was her way of testing me! My thoughts galloped uncontrollably to the off-campus love nest Babs and I would soon establish.

In the midst of February's gloom I started calling the Glockenspiel's. The first few times, the maid answered, causing me to slam the phone down. When I finally got Babs on the line, she made hasty chit chat about renovating the kitchen, without a trace of the emotion I had been waiting for. My imaginary castle was falling down around me and with it my princess. She asked me if I was studying hard.

"I miss you," I said in a hoarse voice.

"Oh Andy," she said, "none of that. I forbid it. Go out and find yourself a nice college girl." And now it seemed *she* was choking up. "And please, Andy, don't call any more, okay?"

I fell into silent desperation. There had been vague invitations for me to return to the Glockenspiels for Spring break, and that was where I pinned my hopes. I prayed Carl would have another appointment at The Hague and my happiness would be restored in another madcap farce of musical beds. But the invitation to the Glockenspiels was withdrawn, Isaac explaining that his parents were taking him to Italy. Nor would I be able to see them during the summer. I already had a summer job lined up in the Midwest.

The weeks rolled on, my tender heart trying to heal itself. Now that I was almost part of the family, Isaac favored me with sneering reports on the bit of fluff — "she ordered a Sauterne with steak!"— to which I would have to force a chuckle. I swore off women, and began to take comfort in the asexual nature of my relationship with Zoë. Now, I was outdoing Zoë herself in mocking the bourgeois complacency of campus heterosexuals. Zoë misinterpreted my new cynicism as the ultimate byproduct of her own jaundiced view of "conventional" society. She considered the New Me to be a creature of her own making, and paradox-

Elated By Details

ically became rather possessive. "Are you 'getting' any?" she would ask me, with mock bravado. But damn me if she didn't seem secretly pleased at my negative answer.

Final exams cut these developments short. In the confusion of year-end parties, packing, and storing, Zoë and I never found time for a private goodbye. I spent a summer of crushing boredom cataloguing new acquisitions in the library of a small liberal arts college near Chicago. The highlight of my day was lunch, consisting of egg salad sandwiches, peppered with the junior librarians' critique of the Australian cinema.

Somehow I tore myself away and made it back to college in plenty of time to lord it over the freshmen. Isaac and I met, by chance, at the campus bookstore. He was wearing an Izod shirt and a look of severe preoccupation. He pulled me aside.

"It's about my dad's wife," he said. "She's pregnant."

"Oh." I stood rigid, mentally bracing myself for scandal, shouting, divorce, a shotgun wedding, expulsion from school, and pistols at dawn. An off-campus love nest with Babs was one thing — but a baby! When I could finally focus on what Isaac was saying, it became clear Isaac's anger was directed, not at me, but at what he took to be his father's irresponsible conduct in siring a child at his advanced age. Even more distasteful, as far as Isaac was concerned, was that the baby was due any day now, meaning Barbara must have got pregnant around New Years, when Isaac was under the same roof.

Adam Freedman

Andrew — aside to audience: I'll say she did!

Isaac went on. At first, the pregnancy had been kept hush-hush. But as they got closer to the date, and as the tests established the presence of a healthy boy, Carl had decided to make the whole thing into a production — complete with lavish showers for Barbara, a major redecoration of the house, and so on — all in celebration of his continued virility. The *pièce de résistance*, as it were, would be the boy's bris, to which simply everybody would be invited.

"Barbara asked me to invite you, so I'm sorry to do this to you. Would you mind coming in for the bris?"

As it happened, Babs gave birth a few days later, and the bris, happily enough, fell on a Sunday. In the meantime, I had reestablished contact with Zoë. Over coffee at Beth's, I explained that I would be going into "the City" for the weekend.

"No way!" she cried. "So am I! I'm going to a play with Liz," she said, naming one of her friends from the literary magazine. "I'm staying over Saturday night. Let's do something on Sunday." The bris was in the morning, so I arranged to meet her at lunchtime. We would have a picnic in Central Park.

The bris was at the Glockenspiel's apartment. The operation itself took no time at all, and left the guests in a kind of deflated empathy with the guest of honor — whose name was Stephen. The party threatened to end in disappointed expectations, but where Carl really outdid himself was the *après bris*. The dining room table, around which guests now

Elated By Details

began to congregate, was groaning under the weight of a catered brunch. There was smoked fish, kosher chicken, and beef tongue, as well as white asparagus points that I considered tasteless in more ways than one.

I elbowed my way through the distinguished-looking crowd to get a look at Stephen, now calming himself down after the traumatic main event. Although I had fancied myself as being prepared for anything, the sight of the baby sent me reeling. I felt joy, terror, awe, and jealousy all rolled into one. This was flesh of my loins. What the hell was I going to do?

My guts were still tying themselves up in knots when, several minutes later, Carl clapped his hand on my shoulder. "Nice of you to come down for this, Andrew. Means a lot to me and Barbara."

I cleared my throat. "Wouldn't miss a ritual mutilation for the world," I said, and instantly regretted it.

"Mutilation?" said Carl. "That's rather harsh, Andrew. I think it's traditions like this that bind a community together, don't you? It's your tradition, too."

"Oh, I'm a devout atheist," I said with a savoir-faire that made me want to kill myself.

"I respect that, Andrew. But circumcision is a pretty widespread procedure, even for atheists."

"But don't you think doing it this way is rather primitive; pagan even?" During this exchange, I had adopted a kind of New England drawl in an attempt to sound extra-collegiate. Would no one stop me?

"Well don't worry about it being primitive, Andrew. We hired the best mohel in New York. Believe me — ho, ho — they don't come cheap."

"I thought they only took tips."

Carl walked away shaking his head while the other nearby guests simply avoided making eye contact with me. Thankfully, Isaac was nowhere to be seen. Babs, however, had been standing nearby. "Oh Andy," she said. "I'm just going to check on Stephen's dressing. Would you be an angel and help me?" When we got inside one of the guest bedrooms, she put Stephen down, sighed, and asked me why I was being such an ass.

"Isn't it obvious?" I said, lips already beginning to quiver. "That's my son! Can't you see what I'm going through?"

"What *you're* going through!" She shook her head angrily. "And what makes you so sure Stephen is your son?"

"The timing! I mean, it's almost exactly nine months since we were, you know, together."

"Andrew, calm down. Carl came back the day after you left."

"Oh great! So you went straight from me to him?"

"I have been known to make love to my husband." Her eyes were hard.

"Love!" I spat, with indignation, but I was beginning to feel a contrary emotion — the heart lightening at the thought of being off the hook for this little bundle of dilem-

Elated By Details

mas. "So, you mean, he's not my son?"

"I don't know," she said. "I'll probably never know."

Now I was miserable again. "What are we going to do?"

"Nothing," she said firmly. "Carl thinks Stephen is his son and that's the way it's going to stay."

I was determined to dig myself in deeper. "So, like, I don't have any say in the matter?"

Stephen began one of those howling baby fits. Babs took him in her arms. I had never seen a woman's expression change so completely; all at once, she was a vision of patience, adoration, and quiet resignation. Her face conveyed truths I could only dimly perceive: unplanned motherhood; unconditional love; a career abandoned; a husband who was both hateful and completely necessary for her son's future; exasperation at this simpering 19 year-old.

"Babs, I'm sorry. It's just — I don't know."

Now she allowed herself a smile. "Look at my two babies," she said. "You can't both cry at the same time. Dry your eyes, Andy. Didn't you tell me you had a picnic to go to? I'll have the maid wrap up some of that food for you. There's enough to feed an army."

That was the last I saw of Babs for some years. I made the short walk to Central Park, my head spinning and my arm weighed down with a hamper full of kosher goodies. It was one of those perfect September afternoons, the air poised between summer and fall, between fecundity and nostalgia. Zoë spread out a blanket in a shaded corner of the Great Lawn and launched into a critique of the play she'd been to the previous evening.

"Was it one of those Sapphic things?" I asked, when she paused for breath.

"No," she said demurely. "I think that phase is over."

She went on talking. The events of the morning began to fade from my consciousness like a bad dream and, like a bad dream, were being replaced by an equally strong sense of well-being. Oh yes, I would agonize over little Stephen's paternity from time to time, but even that would eventually fall into some sort of perspective. I had made a huge deposit into the experience bank, the interest from which would keep me in metaphorical beer and skittles for years.

I was hungry. I had refused to eat anything while inside the Glockenspiel's on the theory that accepting Carl's hospitality would amount to an endorsement of his marriage to Babs and this continuing state of affairs in which I was to be regarded as a youngster rather than an adult. I fiddled with a Tupperware bowl that turned out to have smoked tongue in it.

Zoë sipped wine while explaining she had "exaggerated the whole lesbian thing" and, perhaps, over-estimated the importance of sexual preferences in general. "I have a new theory of identity," she said.

"What's that?"

"You are what you eat."

"Really?" I sidled closer to her, Tupperware in hand. "Would you like some tongue?"

Elated By Details

She turned her face to mine. "I thought you'd never ask, you devil you."

FOLLOW THE BURSTING BUBBLE

I. Monday, January 3, 2000
NASDAQ Composite: 4,131

New Yorkers could not remember a better New Year. The streets were cleaner, the shops more elegant, and the people richer than ever before. The "experts" who had predicted a Y2K apocalypse had turned out to be cranks. Instead, the turn of the century had simply been an occasion for Christmas bonuses that were bigger than ever — checks printed on heavy paper, bearing large round, Rubenesque figures. You could deposit a check like that, button up your coat, and trawl the avenues with intent to purchase. If you were lucky, you might even run into the President's ex-mistress.

Elated By Details

Next January was going to be even better. It was technology, of course, that brought about this rising tide of prosperity. Few people guessed the rising tide had already begun, slowly, imperceptibly, to turn. But it had. And it all began on that first Monday in January, with two men standing in front of a personal computer.

One of them — the young one, the one wearing a bright red shirt — was trying to make a sale. "And if you buy one this week," he said, "we'll include a free Internet access package. It's really fast, especially with a DSL connection."

The other man, tall and wearing a parka that was still zipped up, frowned. "What does DSL mean, anyway?"

The red shirt pretended not to hear the question. The fact is, he'd only been working at Staples for a few weeks — hired for the Christmas rush, but with the promise of a permanent position — and hadn't had time to do more than memorize a few stock phrases. Besides, when it came to the Internet, he had never wanted to learn all the jargon that seemed to go with it.

What was DSL? The red shirt considered making something up. In a pinch he was pretty good at that. Dilithium Series Link? Diaphanous System Logic? No.

"Hello?" said the customer. "I said: what does DSL mean?"

This guy was trouble. And he wasn't going to buy anything; not even the small package of Post-its he was carrying and that he obviously felt gave him the right to harass innocent salesmen. "Basically," the red shirt said, "DSL means faster and more reliable Internet service."

"I mean," said the customer, "what does DSL *stand* for?"

Oh, God. And now another customer was waiting for him, hovering just behind the Christmas display. "If you look at this demonstration," the red shirt said, fiddling with the computer, "you'll see how it works. We've got this model hooked up with a fast modem. You just click here and it takes you right to a customizable web page." He clicked and a new screen appeared:

This Page Has Expired

The red shirt was not prepared for this. He searched the monitor for some clue as to how to proceed. At the top of the screen, there was row of icons, each of which seemed to possess a peculiar sense of urgency: Stop! Refresh! Go Back! Funny, those were all the things he wished he could do with his own life.

"Just a sec, we'll get this straightened out." He could feel eyes burning in the back of his head. "I think you click here, er, no."

"Well, if you don't even know what DSL means—"

The second customer emerged from behind the Christmas display. Although he looked vaguely familiar, the red shirt could not place him.

"Allow me," the second customer said, seizing the mouse. With a click, drag, and click, he got the desired web

Elated By Details

page. "And by the way," the second customer said to the first, "DSL stands for Digital Subscriber Line, okay? Dude, are you going to buy anything? Because I am."

The man in the parka mumbled something rude and wandered away. The second customer turned from the computer. "Hi, I'm looking for a laptop for. . .Hal? Hal Lerner?"

"That's me," said the man in the red shirt — "Hal." The customer affected both surprise and pleasure at this, but was not wholly convincing on either front.

"Rabbi Lerner's son, right?"

"Yes. And you are—?"

"Rob Stephenson. Dude, we went to high school together, remember?"

"Oh yeah," said Hal, reaching out to shake Rob's hand, "of course I remember." When he worked at the bookstore, Hal could go years without seeing anyone from Great Neck Country Day, the slightly shabby prep school to which his father was attached as rabbi and history teacher. But now that he had a truly demeaning job, without even the intellectual pretense of the bookstore, Hal was on a roll. Two weeks earlier he'd run into Toby; and now Rob. He would probably meet another Great Neck alumnus soon: bad things came in three.

"Sorry, Rob," he said. "I didn't recognize you in the business get-up" — suit with four-button jacket, black shirt, no tie — "it's been a while."

"Seven years since graduation," said Rob. "We used to call you 'Slow Lerner,' remember that?"

"Oh. Yeah."

"But that was because of sports, not that you were dumb or anything. Where'd you go to college again? I had you pegged for one of those Ivy League schools."

In fact, Hal had gone to a state college, even though he'd been admitted at Amherst. His father's job got him free tuition at prep school, but not at college. "I went to SUNY-New Paltz," he said.

Rob screwed up his face. "Why'd you go there?"

"I had a Lerner disability."

"I'm sorry."

"It's a joke."

"Oh. I get it. Like 'Slow Lerner.' Dude, you were always a funny guy. So, you're in sales, huh? That's cool."

Hal hadn't thought of himself as being "in sales." That sounded too much like a career. Hal was just waiting for a chance to pursue a better job, or maybe even his secret dream of a Masters in Library Science. He shrugged.

"I mean," Rob continued, "you must learn a lot in a place like this. Like, what's really hot in software and 'net' access packages, and stuff like that."

"I haven't worked here very long."

"Dude, a week is an eternity on the 'net.'"

"Do you work for an Internet company?" Hal asked, genuinely interested. Even Hal found the dot-coms somewhat tantalizing — all those stories of overnight millionaires, kids working in their parents' garages, and soaring stock markets.

Elated By Details

"Venture capital," Rob said smoothly. "We fund the dot-coms." Rob explained that he got his MBA a couple of years earlier. Then he got really lucky when a spot opened up at Tech Ventures, the hottest venture capital firm in Silicon Alley. They always got in at the very beginning of a deal — that meant the biggest risks, but also the biggest rewards. Rob said it was called "angel financing."

Rob summed up triumphantly: "It was Tech Ventures that got metric-now.com off the ground."

"?"

"Dude, where have you been? It is *the* website for everything metric. Metric conversion tables, the history of the metric system, you name it. We're looking at a market cap of 500 million, and I'm getting a piece of that. So, like, how much do you make?"

"Excuse me?"

"Oops, personal question. My girlfriend, Sofia, says I shouldn't do that. But, whatever, I'm guessing twenty, maybe thirty thousand?"

"Maybe," Hal said, and was annoyed at himself for saying as much.

"And you've got a son, right?"

"How did you know that?"

"Let's take a look at those laptops," said Rob. "I have to get Sofia a little Y2K present." Hal led them to a display of laptop computers.

Rob looked at a few computers. "Do you live around here?" he asked.

"In Brooklyn," said Hal. "How do you know about my son?"

"Dude, chill out. I talked to Toby the other day — he gave me the update on you. The truth is, it's not a total coincidence, my running into you here. When Toby told me what you were doing I thought: here's a guy who should get into dot-coms."

"Are you kidding?"

"No," said Rob. "You'd make a lot more money."

"I don't need more money," Hal lied.

"Come on, everyone needs more money."

"It doesn't matter. I don't know anything about dot-coms."

"Good. That's what I need, a totally fresh perspective. There are too many 'angel' dollars floating around, and not enough good ideas," Rob said. Rob explained that he was looking for something new, something that would make him a leader in the "angel community." Hal tried to picture the angel community, complete with angel shopping centers and angel school boards. "The great thing about you being in sales is that you're so in touch with the end user."

"You're wasting your time," said Hal.

"You'd be surprised. Why don't we have dinner and bounce some ideas around? You've probably got ideas you don't even know about. Everything's moving so fast out there, you never know where the next idea is going to come from — you may end up with a piece of the action. Anyway, dinner's on me, so it's a limited downside for

Elated By Details

you. What d'ya say?"

It seemed easier to accept than to refuse. They arranged to have dinner on Thursday and, as Rob made motions to leave, Hal remembered he was supposed to be a salesman. "What about that laptop for your girlfriend?" he asked.

"Laptop? Oh, sorry, dude. Sofia wants one of those really cool, super thin ones. Any idea where I can get one of those?"

After Rob left, Hal was accosted by his extremely fat boss, Oscar. Or Bosscar, as Hal had taken to calling him lately.

"You wanna talk to your friends?" Bosscar said, his breath smelling of gyros and stale cigarettes. "How 'bout you do it on your own time?"

"He was going to buy a computer," Hal said.

"What happened? You talked him out of it? Good work, Hal."

* * *

Later that day, in a downtown loft space, Tech Ventures had its weekly staff meeting.

The Chairman, a man so promiscuous with angel financing he was simply referred to as "the Angel," was sitting at the head of a large, brushed stainless steel table laden with high-caffeine sodas, protein bars, and health waters. The Angel wore a lime-green, Thomas Pink shirt, hunting jacket by Purdy, and aftershave by Penhaligon. Although he had never been to England — friends told him it wasn't worth it — the Angel was a great supporter of the British economy.

Along the exposed-brick walls, frosted glass shelves displayed dozens of acrylic "tombstones," the mementos of Tech Ventures' greatest IPO's: naked people.com, offal.com, hypochondriac.com, paperclip-source.com, and — the Angel's favorites — iHate.com and iLove.com — launched on the same day.

Around the conference table sat the associates of Tech Ventures, young men and women barely able to conceal their terror in the presence of the notoriously capricious Angel. The exception was Rob Stephenson, who appeared cool as he breezed in late, grabbing a Jolt Cola off the table.

"Okay," said the Angel. "I'm listening. Who's got a good idea?"

The associates began competing for the Angel's attention. Tiny microphones picked up their words and fed them into a voice recognition program. A simultaneous transcript of the meeting scrolled up a screen behind the Angel's head.

The meeting did not last long. The Angel firmly believed he had a "feel" for the right ideas and, for three years running the market had rewarded his instincts handsomely. This particular day he rejected most of the ideas; except Levine's project for a lonely hearts website for single accountants. And then Johnson spoke up. Poor Johnson; he wanted to get funding for a group in Colorado that was developing the next generation of co-axial cable.

Elated By Details

"Cable?" the Angel shrieked. "That is so Old Economy. Have you ever heard of fucking wireless?"

"Yeah, I know," said Johnson. "But people are still going to need cable for all kinds of things. This will be a better kind of cable."

The Angel shook his head. "I've warned you about this kind of shit before. You're fired. Get out of here."

After Johnson left the room, the Angel smiled and said. "Now, does anybody else have anything — anything *new*?"

"I do," said Rob, solemn as a bridegroom. "I made contact with that guy I told you about last week. He's got some incredible ideas. No pie-in-the-sky stuff; this dude is totally in touch with the end user."

"Interesting," said the Angel. "Give me more information. What kind of ideas are we talking about?"

This was the tricky part. But Rob had spent much of the last year practicing the tone of voice that implied details were not important. "He's working on a number of Internet applications that are going to anticipate demand months or even years down the road. This dude is gonna change the way people think about the 'net.'"

Now the Angel was interested. "Remind me: what's this guy's name?"

"Hal Lerner."

"Where is he now?"

"He's on the sales and distribution end of tech," said Rob.

"What? You mean he's into *products*?"

"Not exactly. It's kind of an Old-Economy-meets-New-Economy operation."

"Clicks and bricks?" said the Angel. "That kind of thing?"

"That's right."

"I get it," said the Angel, nodding slowly. "His current bosses are obviously too stuck in the past to appreciate the guy. Lerner's into clicks, but his bosses are still into bricks. They obviously had a big falling-out. When did it happen?"

"I'm not sure."

"Find out. Timing is everything with a guy like Lerner. I have a feeling about him. He's learned from the mistakes of the Old Economy and he's ready to join the New. He's got the ideas, but he needs a backer; somebody forward-looking." Rob relaxed, the Angel was on autopilot. "In my experience," the Angel continued, "a guy like Lerner gets financing within about three weeks. Let's get him in here as soon as possible."

* * *

Over in Brooklyn, Hal was paying the baby-sitter, who said she could not work late on Thursday, the night of Hal's dinner with Rob. "Maybe your parents can help?" the baby-sitter suggested.

"Maybe," said Hal, his mind quickly playing out the conversation with his parents, Rabbi and Mrs. Lerner of Great Neck, New York.

Elated By Details

Hal's son, Paul, cried out from across the room. "Daddy!"

"Did you hear something?" Hal said to the sitter. Repeating a familiar gag, he pretended to scan the apartment. "That's weird. I heard a voice, but I don't see anyone."

Paul rushed over to Hal and tugged at his trousers. "Dad-dy! It's me! Look at my drawing!"

After the sitter was gone, Hal knelt down at Paul's play table and looked at the drawing. "Choo-choo," said Paul, pointing to a figure that might have been a train.

"Where's the train going?" Hal asked, and was immediately sorry he had.

"To see mommy," said Paul.

It was almost six months since Susan had left them. After two and a half years with the baby, she had wanted to get her journalism career back on track. Hal had supported her. It was simply a matter of going back to their original plan of putting each other through grad school. He'd never forget the day Susan was accepted to Columbia's journalism school. They drank champagne, undressed each other, and made love the way they used to when they first met.

But it was at Columbia that Susan met Charlie Lovejoy, a visiting professor from Australia. Charlie was always there, at the loud Columbia parties to which Susan used to drag Hal. One day, Susan stopped taking Hal to the parties. She started working on "class projects" that seemed to take until the wee hours. Three weeks after she disappeared —

three frantic, sleepless weeks — a postcard arrived at the apartment.

Dear Hal,

I've moved to Sydney with Charlie. It's beautiful here, but nobody really says throw a shrimp on the barbie or anything like that. Anyway, obviously I think this is for the best or I wouldn't have done it. Give Paul a kiss. I'll write a long letter soon, if I can get Charlie to stop groping me for two minutes! Love, Sue

Susan never did write that long letter. A few days after Christmas, a "Seasons Greetings" card did arrive, with a return address in Sydney. After Paul went to sleep, Hal sat in the kitchen drinking a beer and staring at the card. He pulled out one of his own all-purpose Holiday cards, smoothed out the crease and started to write.

"Dear Susan." Yes, Susan, not Sue or Susie. And he would sign it Hal, not Prince Hal, or Hotspur, or any of the pet names she had dreamed up in college. What else?

Hal finished his beer and wrote: "Thanks for the card. How are you?" For some reason, the effort of writing those few words exhausted him. He took one more look at Paul and went to bed.

* * *

On Thursday evening, Hal met Rob at a restaurant on Avenue B. The walls were dark blue and the chairs uphol-

Elated By Details

stered in a bright orange fabric. Rob was a bundle of energy, jacked up on some new brand of Paraguayan soda and eager to remake Hal into an entrepreneur. "Dude," he said to Hal, "all we need is one good idea."

Hal ordered a bottle of Japanese beer. "I'd love to help, but if I had a lot of great ideas, I probably wouldn't be working at Staples."

"A lot of people started as salesmen," said Rob. "Wanna know why? Guys like you are right there on the front lines. You have got the key to that hidden demand out there in the market. Just think: what are your customers demanding?"

"Refunds."

"Dude, you're killing me."

But even as Rob forced a chuckle, Hal was doing his best to be serious. "Well, our customers want office supplies; you know, computers, printers, paper. I guess you could sell that over the Internet. Would you be interested in some kind of online store, like Amazon, but for office products?"

"The problem with that," said Rob, dipping a mango chip into the salsa, "is that the whole idea is too tied up with physical products. You got to store 'em, pack 'em, ship 'em. And you got to put a value on the inventory and depreciation and all that stuff. Believe me, *products* really fuck up a balance sheet."

"I see," said Hal, taking another slug of beer.

"Don't be discouraged," said Rob. "Listen to this—" To provide inspiration, Rob launched into a description of some of the more recent dot-coms start-ups. There was, for example, the explosive growth of pancake.com, which was already expanding to cover waffles and crepes. There was chewthefat.com, which would soon have voice-recognition technology to allow lonely users to engage in conversations on any number of subjects with the computer. Finally, there was hypochondriac.com, with its hyperlinks to major pharmaceutical companies, which would soon be printing money.

"When you look at companies like that," said Rob, "just ask yourself, what's the next thing?"

"Maybe a dot-com just to keep track of all the other dot-coms," Hal said with a smirk.

"What?" said Rob, looking up from his plate. "Say that again."

Hal assumed an extra-serious expression to keep himself from laughing. "A dot-com to track all the other dot-coms."

"You mean, like, develop all the new dot-coms?"

"Yeah. Develop them."

"I hear you," said Rob. "Some kind of an online, interactive thinkubator. A dot-com of dot-coms, right?"

"Oh, more than that," said Hal, who was finally beginning to enjoy himself. "A thinkubator that thinks about other thinkubators."

"Dude, this is awesome. You're taking the whole thing to the next level. This one totally goes to eleven."

"What?"

"You know, like in *Spinal Tap*? All the other amplifiers

Elated By Details

go up to ten, but this one goes to eleven."

Hal nodded. Was now a good time to tell Rob he had only been joking? No.

Rob stuck with the idea — whatever it was — through dinner. He swore Hal to secrecy and set up another brainstorming session. "If this thing takes off," Rob said as he got into a taxi, "it's bye-bye Staple for you!"

At home, Hal stared at his card to Susan. He composed another line; not strictly true, but close enough. "Guess what? I'm being head-hunted by a dot-com."

* * *

Over the next few weeks, Hal managed several more brainstorming sessions with Rob, stealing away during lunches and a phony doctor's appointment. For Hal, the meetings became an interesting game of semantics. He memorized various high-tech phrases, ascribing what he considered plausible definitions to them, and then experimented with the phrases in conversation. Rob grew ever more dependent on Hal's advice.

"Dude, I'm worried about the cost structure of this thing."

"The costs," Hal said confidently, "are scaleable."

"Yeah, you're right. But how do we stream the data?"

"Uplink?" Hal suggested.

"I guess," said Rob, scratching a memo into his Palm Pilot. "I'll get the tech guys to look into it."

Hal proposed a method for organizing data within the website, using alpha-numeric identifiers to make sure related content remained linked. Rob was overwhelmed, saying he'd never seen such an organizational system. That did not surprise Hal. It was the Library of Congress catalogue system.

By this time, Hal had given up on any notion of a "piece of the action" or "bye-bye Staples." But he did derive one practical benefit from his meetings with Rob. At one point, Hal had mentioned it would easier for him to get away for "business lunches" if Tech Ventures would actually buy something from Staples. Rob made a note and the next day, the office manager for Tech Ventures ordered several new laser printers and a hundred mousepads.

Hal began to set his sights on the Assistant Manager position at Staples: $40,000 and a good health plan. It was a modest goal, but it made him happy — so long as he didn't compare it to the goals he had had before Susan left him.

Through some mysterious alchemy Rob and Hal teased an idea out of their brainstorming. The new venture would be called "meta-dot.com." It would be a dot-com that towered above all other dot-coms, providing some as-yet unspecified thing of value in return for some as-yet unspecified price. Rob was immensely pleased. Of course, the business model had to be refined a little, but that's what angel financing was for.

"And now," Rob said one afternoon, dunking a biscotto into his chai latte, "it's time for us to see the Angel."

Elated By Details

* * *

During one of Hal's brainstorming sessions with Rob, Rabbi and Mrs. Lerner had taken Paul to FAO Schwarz, where Paul fell in love with an $800 toy train.

Hal knew something was wrong when Paul demanded to know when "his" train would arrive at the apartment. When Hal called his parents, his mother confessed she had made some vague promises. "But don't worry," she said, "we'll pay for it."

"No you won't!" said Hal, and slammed down the phone.

Paul burst into tears when Hal told him he could not have the train he saw at FAO Schwarz. When Hal tried to explain, it only made Paul hysterical. Hal wasn't sure how either of them survived the next 20 minutes, but at length Paul calmed down and returned to his toys. Hal watched him playing; his tiny brain processing the idea that other little boys could have things he could not.

The card to Susan was still on the kitchen table. Hal now inserted the word "belated" between Happy and Holidays, and then added another sentence to his message: "In fact, I'm joining a start-up company."

* * *

They found the Angel in the loading dock of the old warehouse that now contained Tech Ventures' offices. He had just taken delivery of a 20-foot-long yellow submarine.

"Gift from my girlfriend," said the Angel. "A personal submarine — it works and everything." It was the least his girlfriend could do, having been favored with a $10 million slice of the metric-now.com IPO. Although the sub was originally delivered on Christmas, the Angel had sent it back so a small cigar humidor and special air filter could be installed.

"I love cigars," said the Angel. "And vintage port, too. Vintage port kicks ass."

Rob and Hal followed the Angel around the submarine, which was cradled in a dry-dock apparatus. "This is the guy I was telling you about," Rob said, slapping Hal's back. "This is Hal."

The Angel turned around. "Good to meet you, Al."

Rob cleared his throat. "You ready to hear the proposal?"

"I'm all ears," the Angel said, and then, turning to Hal, "Half the battle in this business is being a good listener, Al. The problem with the old farts in the brick and mortar companies is that they never listened."

Rob launched into the meta-dot pitch. The future of the Internet, he declared, lay in the B2B business model. And what was the fastest-growing business sector? Dot-com's, of course. What was needed was a dot-com that would organize, categorize, empower, and capitalize on the explosion of dot-com start-ups.

Rob continued talking and the Angel climbed up the dry-dock ladder and got into the submarine. Rob raised his voice, hoping the sound would carry through the slightly open hatch. There was no evidence it could.

The Angel was happily testing the submarine controls. The rudder swung back and forth and the diving planes up and down.

"Turn the flippers twice if you can hear us," said Hal.

"Shhh!" said Rob. But even Rob grew impatient as the Angel lit up a cigar inside the submarine. "It's called meta-dot!" Rob yelled. "Meta-dot-dot-com!"

The submarine hatch opened and the Angel's head poked out. "Meta-dot?"

Rob smiled. "You like it?"

"Love it," said the Angel. "What does it do, again?"

"It combines the depth of the Internet with the breadth of the dot-com revolution—" Hal winced; it had been the other way around when they rehearsed it. "It's going to change the way people think about the 'net.'"

"Cool," said the Angel, now climbing down from the submarine. "What do you need to get started?"

Rob shrugged. "I thought, you know, about two million for the start-up phase."

"Two million? What kind of message are we sending to the market? Let's say four million. I assume Al is going to be C.O.O.?"

Hal looked over his shoulder, searching for the mythical "Al."

"That's right," said Rob.

"Okay, Al," said the Angel. "We'll start you at

$100,000."

Hal thought he had misunderstood. "What?"

"Fine, make it $150,000 — let's not get into a whole thing about compensation. Your real comp. comes with the stock and options when we go IPO. And get us some office space, something cool and downtown. Start looking right away, before rents go up again — let's not waste money!"

* * *

Hal was late getting back to Staples, but there was no problem with the boss. Tech Ventures had placed another large order for office supplies, which put Bosscar in the good graces of the Regional Director. Hal was now a shoe-in for Assistant Manager.

Of course, Hal could quit now if he wanted, and take the job at meta-dot. The only problem was that meta-dot could not possibly last more than a few weeks. It wasn't a company, it wasn't even an idea. It was a joke; or rather, the punch line to a joke Hal hadn't quite finished. Yes, the money was tempting. But surely, Staples was a better bet for the long haul.

Hal could still walk away from meta-dot. There was no contract, no real commitment. He felt, if he could just talk to one person with his feet firmly on the ground, it would give him the courage he needed to forget all about meta-dot.

During a break at work, Hal called his father and told him about Rob Stephenson.

Elated By Details

"Sure, I remember him," said Rabbi Lerner. "He was, if you'll excuse the expression, kind of a dumb jock, wasn't he?"

"He's in venture capital now."

"Figures."

Hal explained to his father that Rob was trying to get him involved in a dot-com start-up that had no product, no service, no customers, and no real ideas. He waited for a cold bucket of Talmudic wisdom.

"Holy schmoly," said his father. "Can you get me in on the IPO?"

"What?"

"Hal, when a company goes IPO, the big *machers* always get a certain number of so-called 'friends and family' shares. That way, your loved ones can get in at the IPO price."

"How do you know about things like IPO's?"

"If you called more often — or maybe even came out and had dinner once in a while? Then maybe you'd notice I've been day-trading for months now. These dot-coms are doing great things for my retirement portfolio."

"So, you think I should do this?"

"Remember, Hal, the Talmud teaches us — and here I translate — make hay while the sun shines. So, yes, maybe it's not such a bad idea." Hal pictured his father sitting there, shrugging his shoulders and turning his palms up to Yahweh.

On the subway back to Brooklyn, Hal made his decision. Who was he to say meta-dot wouldn't be successful?

Maybe it didn't matter that meta-dot was an empty husk of an idea. Maybe what really mattered was his parents' retirement account, and the Angel's yellow submarine. Maybe if enough people wanted money badly enough, the rising tide would lift his little boat, too.

Back in his apartment, Hal picked up the still-unsent card to Susan, re-read what he wrote, and tore it to pieces. "Paul!" he called out. "Get your coat."

"Where are we going?"

"FAO Schwarz."

II. Tuesday, February 1, 2000
NASDAQ Composite: 4,051

Meta-dot was hardly a full-time job. During the first week, the lawyers took care of incorporation, bank accounts were opened, and funds were transferred — none of this involved Hal beyond filling out a signature card. In the meantime, Hal kept up appearances at Staples.

By the second week, the real estate agent had found the perfect office space: downtown, in the heart of Silicon Alley. Hal ordered some spartan office furniture and a top-of-the-line computer from Staples, telling Bosscar that it was another one of his corporate clients. Bosscar took Hal out for a beer and talked about the future of the office supply industry.

On the second Friday, Hal drew his first paycheck on the meta-dot account. He stopped at the bank in the morn-

Elated By Details

ing and opened a college savings fund in Paul's name.

The only problem was the reports. The Angel had demanded one thing: that Hal email him a progress report every week. Why can't I just give you a call, Hal had wanted to say. That, however, might have forced him to explain that he had no computer and, therefore, no email. Probably not the right message from a dot-com entrepreneur.

So, for the first couple of weeks, Hal sent his reports from an Internet café, using a temporary account. By mid-February, he finally had the new office set up and could send his reports directly from the meta-dot computer.

But the solution to one problem created another. The process of setting up the office had given Hal enough material to fill a couple of progress reports with more or less accurate facts. Now, he had no idea what to do. Worse, he had no idea what to write.

Rather than miss the deadline for his next report, which might raise the Angel's suspicions, Hal bought a business magazine and plagiarized from various articles about the digital world. That was how meta-dot began to search for the right "content distribution network" to support "streaming and rapid applications processing."

That sounded like hard work, so Hal invented a couple of employees to do it. He reported the hiring of George Ryan — the name of the super of his apartment building —and Ilyoung Kim — the owner of his corner grocery. Admittedly, he was playing on ethnic stereotypes, but an Asian name did seem to lend credibility to a high tech company.

The following Monday, Bosscar took Hal aside. "Hey cowboy," he said, "I just got a call from the personnel department at Tech Ventures. They wanted to know if you had a 401(k) here to roll over to your new account over there. Care to explain?"

And so, it was bye-bye Staples, after all.

After Bosscar fired him, Hal went to the empty meta-dot office. He ate a sandwich at the desk in the reception area and worked on the day's crossword. Right in the middle of 15 down, the front door opened.

"What a great space!" It was the Angel, wearing a full-length black leather overcoat.

"I wasn't expecting you."

"Not a passive investor, my friend," the Angel said. "Besides, it gave me a chance to get out in my new toy."

"You came by submarine?"

"No, not that new toy. My new, new toy. I bought a Hummer last week. Some of my stocks split and I thought: life's too short not to enjoy, you know? Hummer's kick ass."

"They sure do," said Hal.

"Anyway," said the Angel. "I didn't come here to talk. I came to listen. That's how I got to be a leader in the Angel Community: I listen. Tell me what you're doing."

A crossword, thought Hal. And then he thought: I will be fired from two jobs in the same day. That must be some sort of record. He grasped for the only concrete information he had: "Well, between the lease and equipment, and salaries, we've spent about $40,000 so far. The only thing I

Elated By Details

can really add to my last report—"

"You know what I think?" interrupted the Angel. "I think that's *okay*, but most start-ups would have spent three times as much by now. By the way, where are those tech guys you hired?"

"They're out meeting with, um—"

"Vendors?"

"Vendors."

The Angel frowned. "Sign up any customers yet?"

"No."

"Any advertisers?"

"No."

"Got a business plan?"

"No."

"Any idea what the business will do?"

"Still working on it."

The Angel breathed in sharply through his nostrils and looked around the office. After 30 seconds, he finally spoke. "This is all wrong."

Hal was prepared to refund every penny of the $40,000 he had spent. He had no idea what insanity had taken him this far, but obviously the game was up. If it took him the rest of his life, he would repay the money, so long as the Angel didn't have him arrested.

"Look," said Hal, "I've never done anything like this before."

The Angel cut him off. "I know you've never set up an office before. But still, where the hell did you get this furniture, Staples?" He burst out laughing. "Hal, take it from me. I'm in the business of start-ups. What meta-dot needs is a good interior designer. I'll send you one we use at Tech Ventures."

"Thanks," said Hal. "Sorry about the furniture. I'll never buy from Staples again. Promise."

"Forget about it, but get the place re-done quickly. I'm going to Africa on some kind of safari this weekend, and I want the place looking nice when I get back. We'll have a launch party for the website. One other thing," the Angel said, pointing to the desktop, "get a new computer."

"How many gigs?"

"Fuck if I know, but get one of those things with a flat screen." The Angel walked out the door, calling out over his shoulder, "And think about a business plan."

* * *

Two days later, the interior designer arrived. Her name was Wendy O'Shea and she was young and pretty in exactly the way Hal would have expected an interior designer to be.

Hal gave Wendy a quick tour of the office: in the center was a large reception area; on one side a conference room separated by a glass wall; on the other side, a hallway leading to some offices and a kitchen. Hal asked Wendy what she planned to do.

"That depends," said Wendy. "How do you want to *use* the space?"

Elated By Details

"It's the office for a company called meta-dot."

"I know *that*," she said. Hal noticed she had the decisive habit of emphasizing one word every sentence or so. "I mean, what's your *vision*? Take all this space in front, do you want work stations here?"

"Yeah, sure. Workstations sound good."

"But that won't work if you need the space to receive *customers*. Will customers or clients be coming in?"

"I doubt it."

"Do you need to put a mainframe in here?"

"I don't know. How much does it cost?"

"Let's take a step back," said Wendy — Hal could not believe how brisk she was. Brisk and pretty. "Why don't you tell me what the company *does* and we'll take it from there."

"What it does? It does all kinds of things — it's really a new kind of dot-com. It's like an online thinkubator; it's going to harness the power of the Internet — and using rich content — change the way people think about the 'net.'"

Wendy was staring at him. "I don't mean to be rude or anything," she said, "but you're just making that stuff up, aren't you?"

"I am not!" Hal said with surprising force. It occurred to him that Wendy might be spying for the Angel.

"No need to get snippy about it," she said. "You wouldn't be the first of my clients to make it up as he went along." She took measurements of the office in a cold silence.

* * *

Wendy came early the next day. Hal was at the computer — flat screen now. Paul was there, too; playing on the floor.

Wendy carried a large black bag, from which she produced various paint and carpet samples. Hal tried to ignore her as she held the swatches up against the walls.

A copy of *Wired* magazine lay open on the desk — Hal was trying to make up another one of his progress reports for the Angel. He was concerned there might be some logical inconsistency between what he was writing this week and what he put in the previous reports, but he would have to risk it.

"Daddy!" cried Paul. "I want my choo-choo."

Hal went to the closet where he had stashed a few toys. Wendy's coat was hanging up in the closet. It smelled of her perfume. What was he looking for? Oh yes, the toy train. Hal had left the train at home — that would mean a tantrum. By the time Hal got back to the reception area, however, Paul had forgotten about the train. Wendy had given him some of her construction paper and colored pencils, and he was happily doodling.

"Thanks," said Hal. "Look, I'm sorry I snapped yesterday."

"Don't worry."

The tension between them broke; and they set about planning the office decor. Wendy asked Hal about paint and carpeting and made him feel he was making decisions. He

Elated By Details

arbitrarily chose an office to be his. Then Wendy asked whether he had hired anybody to fill the other offices.

"Of course," said Hal, a note of defensiveness creeping back into his voice.

"Okay," said Wendy. "I need to talk to them so I can find out how they want their offices done. What are their names?"

"There's George Ryan, who you may have heard of and, and—" he couldn't remember young Kim's first name, "and Mr. Kim."

"*Mister* Kim?" Wendy repeated, laughing. "Who's that, your Korean grocer?"

To hell with it, Hal decided, it was easier to confess everything. He had four million dollars and no idea how to spend it. He'd lost his day job and there was no turning back. It was unbearable not to share that information with somebody.

After Hal finished confessing, Wendy smiled and nodded her head as though Hal's case was nothing out of the ordinary. "I know some people who can help you," she said. "They're Internet consultants and they can help you generate some buzz for your website."

"How much do they charge?" asked Hal. He was now afraid of spending more of the Angel's money.

"They'll probably do it for some stock options." Wendy wrote down a couple of names with phone numbers and email addresses.

"Thanks," Hal said. "I'll think about it."

"I really think you should meet these guys. It's important that you get a high profile for meta-dot so you can have a good IPO. That's when all those stock options really pay off."

"So you know all about stock options, too?"

"How do you think *I'm* getting paid?"

* * *

Hal arranged to meet Wendy's friends at an Indian restaurant on Sixth Street. Amidst the kitschy decor and high-pitched sitar music, Hal contemplated the problem of how to spend the Angel's money.

The friends arrived on time, and introduced themselves. Zack Ursik was a website designer; roughly Hal's age with thin blond hair, black-rimmed glasses and a pleasantly inquisitive expression. Steve Cantrell was introduced as a marketing expert. He had bright eyes and lots of baby fat. No sooner had he sat down than he asked, "Hey, do you guys mind if I cruise at around nine? There's an *X-Files* party at Mercer Hall."

"Mercer Hall?" asked Hal.

"NYU," said Steve.

Zack explained that Steve was a junior at NYU. "Don't worry," said Zack. "He's already started and sold a successful dot-com: wherearemykeys.com. It's a search engine for people who can't find their keys. It had a massive IPO."

"Yeah," said Steve, with a slightly embarrassed chuckle.

Elated By Details

"I just stay in school for my parents. I, like, paid my tuition in cash. Remember that, Zack?"

"Sure."

They ordered food and launched into a business discussion. Zack said he found meta-dot to be "pretty non-existent" business wise, but that wasn't necessarily the end of the world.

"Let's say the basic idea is a dot-com designed to generate hype and a certain level of support for dot-com start-ups," Zack said. "We'll make it a one-stop shop for investors, tech guys, and journalists; with links to company home pages, publications, analysts reports, job listings and support services. They'll be lots of discussion groups and audio/video streaming."

"You can do that?" said Hal.

"Piece of cake," said Zack. "It's just another website. The trick is getting all those other dot-coms to register with meta-dot for a fee. That's where marketing comes in."

"Yup," said Steve, finishing a bite of chicken tikka. "The bad news is that all the stuff on our site is available elsewhere for free. The good news is, we'll be offering start-ups the chance to take advantage of our unique proprietary technology."

"What technology?" said Hal.

Zack and Steve laughed. "It's kind of a joke," said Zack. "There isn't any technology, but that's what everybody says. You hire a lawyer to apply for a 'business method'-patent, and that becomes your 'patented technology.'

Nobody ever really asks about it, so don't worry."

"The thing is," said Steve, putting on his coat — it was almost time for *X-Files*— "once we get a few companies on board, the others'll follow because they're, like, afraid of missing out. It's like kids with their toys."

Hal was skeptical. "And you really think companies will pay cash to register with meta-dot?"

Steve smiled as he gathered up his Razor Scooter. "That's the beauty. They don't have to pay cash. We'll take payment in stock options!"

III. March 1, 2000
NASDAQ Composite: 4,784

The meta-dot launch party was a great success. The NASDAQ was climbing to 4,800 — roughly twice its level nine months earlier. There was talk of exuberance.

The office looked terrific: lots of maple paneling, chrome accents, ergonomic work stations, venetian blinds of bright red — Staples red, a private joke. Wendy had been in the office most days during the previous two weeks, overseeing the decorators, going for coffee with Hal, and even helping Zack with website design. When the painters were working, she wore faded jeans and gathered her blond hair into a ponytail and was not above getting into a little paint-splatter fight.

There was something about Wendy that made Hal feel a little threadbare and seedy by comparison. Susan used to

Elated By Details

tell Hal how good-looking he was, but then wives were supposed to say things like that. They were not supposed to run away with Charlie Lovejoy.

Hal found Wendy supervising the caterers as they set up a buffet on the conference room table. There was caramelized kim-chi in a Madeira reduction, Kobe beef with a horseradish/avocado sauce, and sushi made from the rarest, most poisonous tropical fish, expertly de-venomed by New York's best sushi chef.

"Too bad I don't eat sushi," said Hal.

"Neither do I," said Wendy with a giggle. For some reason, this small coincidence made Hal deliriously happy.

A noise in the reception area signaled the arrival of a posse of rich dot-comers, collectively dressed in chinos and dark blue shirts over white tee shirts. They made quick introductions and drifted to the free food.

Rob came with his girlfriend, Sofia Gramasch. She was an aspiring dot-com entrepreneur with fanciful ringlets of black hair and an ironically down-turned mouth. She smiled her funny down-turned smile when she met Hal.

"So glad to finally meet you. *Love* your business model."

"Stop flirting," said Rob. "Hey Hal, this place rocks."

Sofia voiced agreement and urged Hal to join her "Silicon Alley Preservation Committee," a group dedicated to protecting the character of the neighborhood against rampant development.

Somebody spotted the Angel's Bentley driving up to

the building, sending a little thrill through the crowd. Moments later, the Angel himself walked through the door, wearing a purple shirt and somewhat improbable silk ascot. Behind him, an assistant wheeled in a bottle of Dom Perignon bigger than Hal's son. "It's called a 'Jeroboam' of champagne," said the Angel. "Wanna know what's cool? It's older than me!"

Sofia latched on to the Angel, with a big down-turned smile and fluttering eyes. "I have got *the* coolest website idea for you," she said. "It's going to make you some serious money."

"About time I made some serious money," the Angel said. "Where's the money come from? Advertising?"

"That's a joke, right?" said Sofia, somehow managing to flutter her eyes, shake her head, smile, and frown at the same time. "Since when are people talking about advertising? That is *so* not my business model."

Rob eventually dragged Sofia into the conference room where the guests were picking at food and playing Silicon Alley party games.

"Let's play Net Worth!" somebody squealed, to general approval. Net Worth was a complicated game of double-bluffing meant to root out the lowest net-worth person in the room. Normally good fun, it all went badly wrong when Sofia tried to humiliate one of the caterers. It turned out the caterer was a friend of Steve's from NYU and had been an early investor in wherearemykeys.com. In fact, she was richer than Sofia.

Elated By Details

"That's cheating!" cried Sofia. "Nobody told me about her."

"Chill," said Rob. "Here, eat something."

"I still win," said Sofia, her mouth full of sushi.

Minutes later, Sofia became violently ill, her face red and grotesquely puffed up. Evidently, her sushi had not been properly de-venomed. Paramedics were called. The party was a great success.

* * *

Wendy stayed after the party to help clean up. Standing in the kitchen, she dried the wine glasses Hal had washed. Then she stood on her tippy toes to put the glasses on the shelf, making her cocktail dress cling in interesting ways and making Hal feel weak at the knees.

Whether or not Wendy was only "in it for the options," as she insisted, she had certainly earned her share: Zack, Steve, the stunning offices. She had given Hal what he needed to make meta-dot into a real company. No, not a real company, but close enough. "I don't know how to thank you," Hal said, as they stood in the kitchen.

"A few more stock options would be nice. Or you *could* try kissing me."

He opted for the latter, and she put her arms around his neck. They stood there kissing for several minutes.

At length, Hal said, "I would invite you to my place, but Paul's there and the baby-sitter. I can't—"

"Shhh," she said, whispering in his ear. "Why do you think I put a sofa in your office?"

Hal led her into his office. He kissed her neck and shoulders and they fell on the sofa, racing to undress each other. They made love urgently, with Hal on top, and then more slowly, with Wendy on top. Afterwards, Hal held her closely; all he could think was: my marriage is dead.

They dressed and Hal walked Wendy home. The brick streets and renovated warehouses of downtown were mainly dark at that hour. Here and there, brand-new millionaires sat in glass-fronted bars toasting their good luck.

After a long kiss goodnight, Wendy smiled and said, "It's funny, isn't it? I mean, we've only known each other for a couple of weeks."

Hal shrugged his shoulders. "Dude, a week is an eternity on the 'net.'"

* * *

Whatever Zack and Steve did, it worked. Meta-dot had a buzz. Once a few prominent dot-coms registered with the website, everybody had to get a piece of meta-dot's "proprietary technology." Dot-coms from around the country — even around the world — were signing up, and they were paying in options. As the NASDAQ rose, now spiking to over 5,000, so did the market value of the options that meta-dot received. On paper, at least, meta-dot was hugely profitable.

Elated By Details

They now had a treasurer —Warren Frankenthaler, Rabbi Lerner's accountant — to tell them exactly how profitable meta-dot was. George Ryan and Mr. Kim were quietly fired. In their place, Zack became Vice President - Operations, Steve was V.P. - Marketing, with a flex-time schedule that didn't interfere with his classes at NYU. They hired an office manager and a few dreadlocked assistants to deal with the mechanics of the website. Wendy's workstations were a big hit.

Hal signed checks and contracts, but otherwise had little to do. He took Paul to see the dinosaurs at the Natural History Museum and to play at Chelsea Piers. He had long lunches with Wendy and took her to Vermont for a weekend.

There was no point in trying to learn the business. Frankenthaler had explained everything Hal needed to know in one brief conversation: meta-dot did nothing and had no assets. It was profitable because it had the right, but not the obligation to buy stocks in dozens of other companies that did nothing and had no assets.

"You know what it's like?" said Frankenthaler. "It's like one of those pyramid schemes my neighbors are always getting into."

At the end of the month, the Angel summoned Hal to his office. Workmen were clustered around the Angel's private bathroom, installing Carrera marble, gold fixtures, and a toilet that measured the user's weight and blood pressure. The Angel stood nearby, wearing a black cashmere turtleneck and talking into a cell phone.

"No way," he said into the phone, "that place is totally unacceptable. For starters, there's nowhere for the helicopter to land. And another thing—"

Two minutes later, the Angel was off the phone and listening to Hal's report. For once, Hal felt completely confident in the Angel's presence. Meta-dot's subscriber base now numbered in the hundreds and, based on the value of the subscribers' stock options, the company was running a large profit. Hal wondered whether he would get a reward — a large bonus or at least a submarine.

Instead, Hal got a scolding from the Angel. "What makes you think this is good news?" he said. "We can't possibly do an IPO under these conditions. Your figures suck."

"We'll try to do better," Hal said quietly.

"You'll have to. Do you have any idea what this kind of profit margin says to the market? It says: this company has peaked, this company spends no money on R and D, this company is stagnating, this company," the Angel shook with a controlled fury, "has an Old Economy balance sheet!"

"I'm sorry."

"You have got to deliver a solid quarter of *losses* before we go IPO, understand?"

On his way out of the Tech Ventures building, Hal ran into Rob. He learned that Sofia's sushi poisoning had been bad indeed. She was now languishing in the tropical disease ward at Johns Hopkins, slipping in and out of consciousness.

Elated By Details

"That's nothing," said Hal. "The Angel just found out meta-dot is making a profit."

"Dude, that sucks. Gotta up the expenses."

Hal returned to the meta-dot offices where he made a surprise announcement: everyone's salary was doubled.

IV. July 3, 2000
NASDAQ Composite: 3,991

As luck would have it, April and May brought a sharp "correction" to the NASDAQ. Nobody cared too much, since it was obviously just the prelude to a massive year-end rally. It did mean the value of meta-dot's portfolio of stock options temporarily plummeted while its expenses were increasing. At long last, meta-dot was losing money. The Angel greeted the news with enthusiasm and an additional $20 million investment in the company.

Now, with the NASDAQ rebounding and confidence back up, it was time to do an IPO. Investment bankers were called in from the firm of Bull Stevens. The bankers were the same age as Hal, and talked like Rob. They wore spread collar shirts and bright ties and kept referring to meta-dot's "present value."

"Present from whom?" Hal asked.

"Good one, dude," one of the bankers said.

The bankers toured the office and inspected the company books. Contrary to Hal's expectations, he was not handcuffed and frog-marched out of the office. Instead, the bankers gathered the meta-dot executives around the conference table and told them the company had a present value of $15 billion. That was based on projected subscriber growth, stock option appreciation, future advertising revenues and, of course, the value of the proprietary technology. Zack gave Hal a wink.

It came as a shock to Hal to learn he had to join the bankers on the "Road Show," a cross-country tour to meet prospective IPO investors. Hal left Paul with his parents and joined the Road Show in Boston.

In a banquet room of the Boston Ritz, a gung-ho managing director from Bull Stevens gave a Power Point presentation about the future of e-business and e-commerce. Meta-dot, he explained, would not just redefine business, it would "e-define" business. Some older companies might be "e-calcitrant" at first, the banker conceded, but meta-dot would lead an "e-alignment" of business models.

When the questions came, Hal kept deferring to Bull Stevens until one of the bankers took him aside. "Dude, you're, like, a visionary, okay? You gotta tell them what your vision is."

"Twenty-twenty."

"What?"

"Never mind." Hal hoped his simplicity would be mistaken for "vision." It seemed to work. When he said he wanted to "harness the power of the Internet," the fund managers nodded approvingly and never asked follow-up questions.

Elated By Details

Rob also went on the *Road Show*, but he spent most of the time on his cell phone, arranging new deals and checking on Sofia, who had now been transferred to the Mayo Clinic in critical condition.

From Boston, they went to Cleveland and then Chicago, always staying in the best hotels and dining at the best restaurants. Hal did some sightseeing, while the bankers spent most of their free time in the hotel health clubs, engaged in a cross-country bench press competition.

Wendy flew out to Palo Alto, where Hal's hotel suite had a private deck with hot tub. She poured him wine and laughed at him. "Can't you even relax in a hot tub? Let me give you a massage. There, that's better. You're going to be rich, silly." They made love, starting in the hot tub and moving to the bed — hot pink skin against fresh white sheets — slowly, and without a thought of neighbors or baby sitters.

The IPO, when it came in late August, exceeded all expectations. The NASDAQ was roaring back, now over 4,000 again. Smart analysts credited meta-dot with sparking the rally and predicted a NASDAQ Composite of 8,000 by year end.

Later, Hal would remember those days as a dream, with day-glo colors and strange voices. There was the sound of his own name on television — "visionary dot-com guru Hal Lerner" — phone calls from old friends and new real estate agents, and a conversation with Warren Frankenthaler.

"What exactly does the IPO mean, Warren? I get some of the stock, right?"

"Based on yesterday's closing price, I'd say about $20 million worth," said Frankenthaler, who was beaming for he, too, had become a meta-dot millionaire.

There was the sound of Susan's voice, long distance from Australia. "Congratulations Hal! That is so great! You see? I always said you could do anything if you really, really set your mind to it. Remember? Remember me telling you that? Anyway, the thing is, I was thinking of moving back to New York—"

And finally, there was the sound of Hal's own voice speaking into the receiver, sounding harder and more certain than it ever had or ever would: "Paul stays with me."

On the last day of August, Sofia lapsed into a coma.

V. September 1, 2000
NASDAQ Composite: 4,234

"You have to learn to enjoy your money," the Angel said to Hal. It's good for your soul. Besides, it projects confidence—we can't have the founder of meta-dot afraid to spend his hard-earned millions."

The following week, the Angel took Hal car shopping: Jaguar, Bentley, Rolls Royce, Rover. The Angel remained steadfast in his support of Pound Sterling. In the Range Rover showroom, Hal gave in to nerves. "I don't know. The NASDAQ's really been sliding the last few days. I'm worried."

"Hal, stocks go down, they go back up. That's what they

Elated By Details

do. What? You're worried that you're only worth $18 million?"

In the end, Hal bought a Saturn. The Angel could live with that. It was like Bill Gates eating at McDonalds: visionaries did things like that sometimes. At least Hal paid in cash, which the Angel considered a nice touch.

To Hal, the modest little Saturn symbolized his ability to keep his head despite all the money swirling around him. He did not keep his head for long. The act of spending money had a way of snowballing. Wendy offered to help him look for a new house. She gently nudged him from Brooklyn to Manhattan, from standard two-bedroom to loft space. Somehow, Hal found himself taking a serious look at a $2.5 million loft in Soho.

"It's really unique, you know?" the real estate agent said, as sunlight poured through the skylight and their footsteps echoed in the vastness.

The agent led them to an oversized bathroom. In the middle of it sat a hot tub — identical to the hot tub in Palo Alto that had been such a high point in their erotic lives. Hal's eyes met Wendy's.

"I know what you're thinking," said the agent. "How can a place like this go for under three mill?"

"Took the words out of my mouth," said Hal. Wendy elbowed him.

The agent looked at Hal. "Talk it over with your wife."

Later, as they sat in a nearby diner, Hal said he couldn't possibly buy the loft.

"Why not?" said Wendy. "It's within your budget. I'll get you a designer's discount on all the furniture. You're a millionaire, silly."

"Today I am. Who knows what's going to happen?" Hal had already had his world yanked out from under his feet once, when Susan left. It was a bad feeling, and he had made it worse by allowing himself to feel so happy with Susan. Happiness was the enemy: it led to disappointment.

"You're thinking of Susan, I can tell. Hal, this is a house. It's a *thing*. You can sell it later if you want. You don't have to trust anybody to buy a thing. You don't have to trust *me*."

"Wendy."

"I'm sorry. I just wish you'd live in the present."

And so, to prove he could live in the present with the best of them, Hal went to the realtors and signed a contract for the loft. He kept repeating to himself: it's only a thing.

* * *

Back at meta-dot, Hal found the Angel waiting for him, propped up against Hal's own desk. "You remember Sofia Gramasch?" he said.

"Yes. How is she?"

"Bad. Dead, in fact. That fucking sushi killed her, and now her family is suing meta-dot."

"Suing us?" said Hal. "But we didn't make the sushi."

"Doesn't matter. She ate the sushi on company premis-

Elated By Details

es and that makes meta-dot liable. Based on the medical bills, and Sofia's future earning potential, plus pain and suffering, the family is asking for five billion." The Angel paused for effect. "This is going to hit the stock hard."

"Oh well," said Hal. "Stocks go down, they go back up. That's what stocks do, right?"

"I don't know what the fuck you're talking about. This whole market's going south, and especially meta-dot. I'm bailing while the shares are still worth something. I just wanted you to know."

"But you're the biggest shareholder," said Hal. "If you sell your shares, that'll kill the price, won't it?"

"Probably. The company's toast."

"Then I'm going to sell my shares," Hal said. "I have a son."

The Angel shook his head. "You can't sell, you're management. Part of the IPO was your promise not to sell any of your shares for two years. You try to sell now and you'll have the SEC and a bunch of angry investors crawling up your ass." The Angel started to leave. "But you're a smart guy — keep in touch and let me know if you have any more of those visionary things."

"Wait, wait, wait," Hal cried out. "Can't you hold off on selling your shares? I just bought a house."

"Big mistake — nobody's buying anything now; everyone's selling, including me. In fact, my real estate agent just called to tell me she dumped my loft on some schmuck for two point five mill!"

Adam Freedman

* * *

The Gramasch litigation inched its way through pretrial procedures during the Autumn. Meta-dot's lawyers managed to hold things up by filing a motion to dismiss the lawsuit. The same lawyers also got Hal out of his new loft. Luckily, the Angel's house had never been zoned residential, allowing Hal to break the contract. In the meantime, however, his landlord in Brooklyn had re-rented his apartment. For the time being, Hal moved in with his parents, which thrilled Paul.

Hal became a commuter, driving his Saturn into the City in the morning, doing what he could to keep the company alive, and then driving home again. He learned Wendy, who was free to sell her stock, had done so. Hal wanted to tell her she did the right thing, but she seemed to avoid his calls, leaving messages explaining she was too busy. When this all blows over, Hal said to himself, I'll take her away for the weekend.

The markets staged a pre-election rally; the NASDAQ rose above 3,400. For a few days, Hal thought he could see light at the end of the tunnel. Maybe the share price would come back; maybe the lawsuit would be dismissed; maybe he could keep the company alive long enough to cash out.

But in November — just when the country was having such a hard time picking a president — the judge decided not to dismiss the Gramasch lawsuit. Meta-dot had no choice but to settle with Sofia's family.

Elated By Details

Friday, December 1, 2000
NASDAQ Composite: 2,645

The settlement negotiations lasted into early December as the NASDAQ struggled to get back to what the papers called the "psychologically important 3,000 level."

Ultimately, the only way for meta-dot to pay Sofia's family was to liquidate its portfolio of stock options — before they lost all their value. Frankenthaler orchestrated a massive sell-off; dumping large chunks of the leading dot-coms.

On Wall Street, the trading desks noticed the selling and, sensing the Fat Lady was finally singing, starting selling all their tech stocks. It was a vicious downward spiral of dot-coms, and meta-dot's own stock was sucked into the vortex. The NASDAQ plunged below 2,400, less than half its level nine months earlier. Billions of dollars of value simply disappeared.

On cable TV, analysts debated whether the sell-off was caused by the uncertain presidential election, or the disappointing earnings reports, or the Fed's refusal to cut rates. Nobody mentioned the sushi.

* * *

Hal was still coming to meta-dot every day, except now he came by train. He'd had to sell his Saturn to pay the meta-dot lawyers for their services in getting him out of his house-buying contract. The cash he got from the car was well short of the $50,000 legal bill, but the lawyers had been gracious in giving Hal a break. Meta-dot had been a good client and, what with the dot-com crash, their bankruptcy practice was exploding.

In the meantime, Hal had not seen Rob in weeks. That was understandable. It would have been impossible to discuss the Gramasch lawsuit while Rob was still mourning Sofia's death. Now that the case was settled, things could get back to normal. When Rob finally did come to the meta-dot office, Hal gave him a friendly hang-in-there greeting.

"Thanks," said Rob. "So, no hard feelings?"

"About what?"

"Didn't Wendy talk to you?"

"No," said Hal. "She's been really busy."

"Oh, shit," said Hal, keeping his eyes fixed on the floor. "The thing is — Wendy and I kind of hooked up at Sofia's funeral, you know?"

"No."

"She really helped me get through, like, the whole grieving thing, and now we're together. Sorry, I thought you knew already."

"I probably should have known, but I'm a Slow Lerner."

"Jeez, I wouldn't say that. I think you're — oh, I get, that's a joke, right?"

"Right."

"It's cool of you to be making jokes and everything. Wendy says that she, like, still really cares about you."

Elated By Details

"That's nice."

"She's great, isn't she? She's decorating my new house. Fuckin' NASDAQ, man. I'm so glad I started selling that crap short six months ago. Hey, speaking of that, did you see that Integrated Systems bought five percent of meta-dot?"

"Huh? Oh, yeah. That's good, right?"

"It's bad. They're bottom fishing. This company's a dud."

"A dud?" Hal repeated, slowly. "Wow, I used to be a dude, now I'm a dud, or at least I work for a dud. I mean, what's the difference? Just one little 'e.' Do you think that's the same 'e' as in e-commerce and e-business and e-tailing?"

Rob eyed him tentatively. "I'm not sure what you mean. Is this, like, another business idea?"

"No. I'm saying that maybe a *dud* is just a *dude* without the e-business. What do you think, Rob?"

"You okay, Hal?"

* * *

Shortly before Christmas, Hal had to let everyone go. Meta-dot's stock had dropped to a few pennies and was delisted by the NASDAQ. There were no subscribers left and no money.

Hal watched as the employees — his employees — packed their boxes and held back tears. They loved Hal and still talked about the day when he doubled everyone's salary. Zack and Steve left much as they had arrived: relaxed and happy, especially Steve, who'd aced his math final.

In the midst of the farewells, five unfamiliar men in dark suits walked through the front door and asked for Hal. They were accountants and lawyers from Integrated Systems. Their employer was insisting on its right, as a shareholder, to inspect the books and records of meta-dot. Hal pointed them to Frankenthaler's old office. Poor Warren, thought Hal, he had given up his accounting practice for meta-dot, and he'd ceased to be a paper millionaire several months ago.

It wasn't until hours after the Integrated Systems people left that Hal started to worry. Why had they sent lawyers? Accountants he could understand, but lawyers? They must be preparing a lawsuit against meta-dot or Hal, or both. Or maybe they would turn Hal over to the government. Surely what meta-dot had done — that is, pretending as though its shares and its services were actually worth something — was some species of crime. People went to jail for things like that.

Hal's worry turned to cold panic when he was summoned to the Integrated Systems office. He trudged through the spongy, slushy streets on New Year's Eve afternoon, arriving at Integrated's headquarters on Lexington Avenue. He was whisked to the General Counsel's office, where the lawyers greeted him with tight smiles and polite handshakes. This, thought Hal, is going to be a lynching.

The lawyers took Hal to a large office where a tall, dour

Elated By Details

man introduced himself as Vice President - Acquisitions. "We want to acquire meta-dot," he said. "Obviously, you don't have any assets to speak of, except your name."

"Hal Lerner?"

"Good to see you've still got your sense of humor," the V.P. said, without himself breaking a smile. "Anyway, you know what I mean: meta-dot achieved something of a brand name status. Someday, the dot-coms will come back, and we want to own that name. We're willing to cash you out of the company at a reasonable premium." The V.P. named a sum that would make a nice down payment on a modest house in Brooklyn.

"There is one condition," the V.P. continued. "You have to agree to work for Integrated Systems, as a consultant, for at least a year. Deal?"

Everything was settled briskly, hands shaken and documents signed. Hal rode the elevator down in a fog; he was so relieved it gave him a headache. It would have been nice to celebrate, but he'd made no plans for New Year's.

* * *

Weeks later, after Wendy's engagement to Rob had been announced and after Susan had returned to New York, Hal settled into his new job. He had a cubicle at Integrated Systems, right next to a guy named Johnson who had been fired from Tech Ventures a year earlier. Hal and Johnson swapped stories about the Angel.

Adam Freedman

One day when work was slow, Hal finally made the phone call he'd been putting off. Sitting in his cubicle, he dialed his father's extension at the History Department of Great Neck Country Day.

"Dad, I wanted to talk to you about this meta-dot disaster."

"Of course, Hal. That was a terrible thing that happened to your company. If there's anything I can do to help—"

"No, that's not what I mean. Look, I know how much you put into the meta-dot IPO. It must have blown a hole in your portfolio. I feel so terrible, but, what does the Talmud say? 'The road goes out, the road comes back—'"

Just then, Johnson poked his head into Hal's cubicle to ask a question. Hal put his hand over the receiver to answer. When he returned to the phone, his father was saying something: "…Rabbi Cohen teaches us the proper valuation of things—"

"Who's Rabbi Cohen?"

"Not 'Rabbi Cohen,' Hal, Abby Cohen. She's the chief analyst at Goldman — really sharp lady. When meta-dot's P/E ratio went over 500, she told everyone to sell. That's the thing, you know? When everybody else is buying, all the smart cookies are selling. I got out at 12; I thought you knew."

"No."

"Oh well, so no harm done. Everything worked out fine for your mother and me. How's your friend Rob?"

"He's getting married."

Elated By Details

"Give him my best wishes, would you? Funny, just the other day, I was trying to remember what Rob was like in high school. He was never the type I thought would be successful in life. There was nothing original about him, you know what I'm saying? He just jumped on to whatever bandwagon was going. I always thought the future belonged to the guys who bucked the trends. Whatever made me think such a load of *mishegaas*, I'll never know." He laughed. "Have you seen Susan?"

"Yes. We're trying to work things out." Susan had surprised Hal. She came back to him knowing he had lost everything. She was supportive and told Hal she longed to rebuild their family. For Paul's sake, they probably would.

"So, Hal, maybe it's none of my business, but did you lose a lot on this meta-dot deal?"

That depended on how you looked at it. Strictly speaking, he was better off than he was a year ago, which was more than a lot of people could say. But there were times when he thought about the money, and the parties, and Wendy, mostly about Wendy. Times when it seemed like a different life had been within his grasp, and then slipped away. Had he lost a lot?

"About twenty million."

"Oy! I had no idea. I'm sorry, Hal."

"It's okay. Really, it is."

"How's my grandson?"

"He's got a new expression: 'easy come, easy go.' God knows where he picked that one up."